PAUL SMITH was born in Manchest
his mother). Having stumbled, som
a state Grammar School at 11, he e'
system of only ever working when a.. _
been exhausted. Late flowering scholastic skills did allow
progress to the sixth form and then University. Qualifying
as a lawyer in the 1980s he subsequently built up a very
successful insurance business. At the moment he is busy
developing a second rapidly growing financial services firm.

Commercial success and its rewards have allowed him
to develop interesting new tastes and both hunting and
shooting have appeared to him as essential and immensely
invigorating ways of living life.

Over the last 25 years or so he has hunted with the crack
Yorkshire hunts (still thriving within the law) and had the
pleasure of joining the Mastership of the Middleton Hunt
in 2009, retiring after four seasons in 2013. He is also
a keen shot, when the Hunt Meet Card allows. During this
25 years the characters in this novel have slowly grown
in his mind. While the tale is set in the 1980s it tells of
a world that only changes very slowly.

The beginnings of the novel itself came when a serious
and very talented literary friend challenged him to turn various scraps and sketches into a full-blown novel. Of course
the tale grew in the telling and the characters developed lives
of their own. So, for the first time, the world of Blankshire
is presented...

Paul Smith

The Owl *and the* Earl

SilverWood

Published in 2014 by SilverWood Books

SilverWood Books Ltd
30 Queen Charlotte Street, Bristol, BS1 4HJ
www.silverwoodbooks.co.uk

ISBN 978-1-78132-255-0 (paperback)
ISBN 978-1-78132-256-7 (hardback)
ISBN 978-1-78132-257-4 (ebook)

THE OWL AND THE EARL

PROLOGUE

The Lesson

"WELCOME, COME IN. Hector Griffiths, if I'm not mistaken? Mind if I call you 'Ector? As the sign on the door will 'ave told you, this is the Albert Holloway Academy of Shootin'. I'm Albert Holloway, and we're open to anyone. Anyone 'oo can afford our prices, least ways. Not everyone it's true, but I'm told you qualify."

Before me was a generously built man, large of frame and well covered. Dressed in a scruffy workaday suit of keeper's tweed, it was clear he did not expect his tailor to speak for him. That he was a man of substance was beyond question, about 240 pounds of substance I'd have guessed.

"The thing is, you don't get many of me to the pound. After all, 'ow many people do you know 'oo knows 'ow to make lilac scented candles, do proper justice to a decent sized slice of roast beef and lay claim to be an international sporting legend and world champion seven times over?"

There was a pause although the question clearly rhetorical.

"Not that many, I'll tell yer."

This bold statement of accomplishment from the mouth of Albert Holloway was what I had been led to expect. I'd been warned he was larger than life, and life seemed quite large enough. Albert was in his mid thirties, a man in his prime and aware of it. His pale blue eyes twinkled with fun and intelligence, and his ruddy cheeks spoke of hours in wind and rain. It is fair to say his personality and stature were made for one another.

"So welcome, young 'Ector, to my shooting academy. Not everyone has the sense to pay my exorbitant prices because people are very reluctant to appreciate that quality 'as a price, both financially and in terms of effort. Now, it just so 'appens to be your lucky day, because you come to me 'ighly recommended by my old friend Hobson, a rogue 'e may be but man and boy I've known him. Because you come 'ighly recommended by 'im, you shall 'ave the first lesson on the 'ouse, a privilege conferred upon very few, I can tell yer. The man 'oo does free around 'ere is usually out, permanently."

He paused, again clearly aware there was no answer to this soliloquy. It had been suggested I go to see this leviathan of the shooting world by my long time business associate, Andy Hobson. Hobson had first met Albert, born the son of a Norwich candle maker and now the seven times recurring world champion at blasting small clay objects to smithereens, some twelve years earlier, and had immediately recognised his talent. Back then, Albert had still been working in the family candle-making business in Norwich by day and tearing around East Anglia in a beat-up old car by night and at weekends, appearing wherever he could find shooting competitions offering cash prizes. As a sideline he developed the handy habit of taking on all comers in high stakes betting. I gather he seldom lost as the subject of the bets was usually based on his ability with his shotgun.

A benign act of generosity and patronage by Hobson in supporting Albert's raw talent had grown and prospered into an abiding friendship: two singular individuals sharing a common love. In turn, I knew Hobson, not from my first, short career as a Master Mariner, but from my involvement in the sometimes murky world of shipping. I had joined the Merchant Navy at seventeen and after 10 years spotted an opportunity to make proper money on shore. It was then I first met Hobson, a self made man who lived on his wits, with which he was abundantly supplied. Recently he had proposed taking over the shipping business that I had spent twenty long, hard years building up, which would mean, in the nicest way, I would no longer be required. Indeed, I was going to be pitched full time into something I understood to be called "leisure time", which was to be a new experience for me. One I thought I was looking forward to.

As a result, I decided I ought to try a range of "leisure related experiences". Hobson suggested shooting might capture my fancy, and that I entrust myself to his Norwich friend.

So here I was, to have a lesson with Albert. Since the early days of successfully potting clays against all comers locally, Albert had developed not only his shooting talents but also his commercial skills. He now ran a shooting school, based on the outskirts of Norwich, not far from the beginnings of the Norfolk Wolds, that was building a good reputation. I had just walked rather sheepishly into the small sunlit shed which masqueraded as the school's office. Outside, the muffled crump and crack of shotguns being used on a variety of clay targets provided a backdrop.

Albert beckoned me to a chair by the desk and resumed my introduction to his world. "Me and Hobson, we goes back an awful long way, and an introduction from 'im is worth a lot in my book. Things around 'im tend to work to our mutual advantage, yer see, so I reckon any friend, any proper friend, of 'is is already a proper friend of mine.

"And I'll tell you this much, young 'Ector, it's good to meet people who are just learning to shoot. And it's nice to meet a Welshie, by the way. We don't get enough of 'em around 'ere. Don't even get many people from Suffolk, although that I *do* understand. Just remember, if we get on together you'll always 'ave a friend to 'elp yer, although why a top geezer like you will ever need any 'elp from the likes of me is anyone's guess. Carry on paying attention like you 'ave so far and I reckon we'll get on like a house on fire. After all, we all like to be listened to.

"Now, you ready for your first lesson?"

ONE

The Pans

I PULLED UP in a crunch of gravel outside the Old Rectory. The Hon Alexander Bicester, technically Lord Blankshire since the recent death of his father but known among us still simply as Alex, was waiting in the porch. We didn't meet unless there was a crisis, as I got out of the car there was only the briefest of greetings.

"Evening, Master Hector," Alex said, before he turned on his heels and walked into the house. Clearly time was not to be wasted.

I scurried obligingly after him through the main door into the hall, and turned right into the large Georgian dining room. The other Masters of the Blankshire Hunt had arrived before me. The door to the kitchen was open, and Charlotte, Alex's wife, stood there. A tall, striking, matriarchal lady in her mid forties, her raven black hair with a scattering of silver piled up in a way that hinted of Cruella de Ville, she was without question an imposing women. There was little doubt as to whose lair I had entered.

"Evening, Hector, I trust you're well?"

As ever, her greeting was short almost to the point of being curt. It was clear that, although not a tradesman, I was not quite an equal either. More a means to an end, and the end in question was the future of the Blankshire Hunt.

Her husband, and my very recently acquired friend, wandered genially around the room, a bottle of wine in his hand. Bluff and craggy, a little stooped although not yet fifty, his smile was genuine and warm, a comfort for the soul against the frostiness of his other half.

"Come in, come in, take the seat by the fire. It's a cold night. Glass of wine for you? Cup of tea? Something to warm the bones? Sorry, bit abrupt earlier. Lots to discuss, need to get on." As ever his generosity was heartfelt.

Charlotte retreated into the kitchen; a cauldron to attend to, no doubt. Besides Alex and myself, the other three Masters of the Blankshire were present. Frank Ramsbottom was a tenant farmer from the moor tops. It is said that genetically these men from the hills, yeoman all, were a race apart, and without question they did usually grow tufts of hair from their upper cheeks. They were also known for their parsimonious ways, both with words and cash, and Frank was true to his breeding.

Then the newest addition to our small team, Lettice Edgerton-Farley, a bright-eyed attractive lady in her late forties, razor sharp of mind and occasionally of tongue. Generally a good sort, she was not to be crossed. She had the ear of everyone who counted in the strange world of county backwoodsman, had the ability, when provoked, to wither grass at fifty paces, and owed neither fear nor favour to any of her peers. This evening she had one small handicap: her mouth opened to articulate a welcome, but no sound emerged. This particular queen bee had lost her buzz! There was a lot of waving and pointing at her throat, and then she held up a sheet of paper in the manner of a very superior TV quiz show contestant.

"LARENGITIS. SORRY!"

Alex intruded into the conversation, or, more precisely, the lack of it.

"Lettice has very kindly agreed to attend this evening even though, as you can see, her ability to contribute is somewhat limited."

Limited? More like non-existent, I thought to myself. But never mind. She was here, and she might be able to nod usefully if it came to a vote, although a vote was pretty unlikely. We didn't really do democracy in the conventional sense; we enjoyed a subtle variation on the one man, one vote norm. Ours was more of the one acre, one vote kind, and as Alex had about 20,000 acres his views tended to prevail.

The final Master was old hand, Philip Quinn-Harkin. A bright and successful local man, Philip was believed to have several virtues, and had been involved in the business of running a hunt for many years. We knew this because he told us so frequently, and whenever possible at some length. His experience was said to count for a lot, especially on the technical and practical side. My limited knowledge of him suggested that he was the type of individual who ached with every fibre of his being to be part of whatever "it" happened to be at any given moment in time. To be a permanent member of the in-crowd was his goal, and at any potential confrontation he was likely to assume a posture of near invisibility.

We settled to the business in hand, wine poured; fire roared.

"To the agenda, Lady and Gentleman." As always, Alex was polite to a fault, conducting this meeting as he would have conducted a meeting of one of his innumerable family trusts. Like a particularly sinuous river we moved slowly across our landscape of responsibilities. Ah, the stuff of which organising the life of a hunt is composed. From the old perennial of hunt horses, either not enough or too many that are broken, through the minutiae of hedge trimming, jump clearing, and bridge installation, we then moved on to the tricky question of the fences down by the brook. I was never quite sure which was the brook in question, but its fences needed to be rebuilt. Finally we arrived at access on to the land of the farming community.

Alex was a master of delegation. Tasks were summarised and parcelled out to others; one could only admire the aplomb with which he identified and delegated responsibility.

"Hector, look, I say, yer know old Smythson up at Batterson Brook? Difficult feller. Could you go up and see him? You're new in the Mastership, not had time to annoy him yet, what?" I knew nothing of Smythson, and only had the faintest idea where Batterson Brook was. At that stage I felt flattered to be asked to help; I had yet to appreciate quite how quickly the chalice could be filled with poison and passed to the most innocent volunteer.

I'd sold my business three years earlier after a protracted financial courtship with friend Hobson, and, relieved of the responsibility, had felt years younger. Before long I'd settled on hunting rather than shooting as my first love. After three seasons of being a regular with the Blankshire I had been asked to join the mastership: the four or five individuals who make up the executive of the typical hunt. Known in this curious little world as a Master of Fox Hounds, or MFH to those involved, I had initially felt rather flattered by the invitation, perhaps even, a little bit important. I quickly realised I had been invited to join this rather exclusive club not because I was a great horseman (I wasn't), or because I had the faintest idea how to help guide the proceeding of a hunting day but because of my financial acumen. However, I was fascinated by the sheer minutiae and domesticity of it all. No lives ruined or jobs lost. Having fled the daffodil valleys of South Wales at the earliest opportunity, I had spent almost half a lifetime building up a large shipping business where big decisions had become routine. By comparison, being a member of the Blankshire Mastership was deliciously reminiscent of running one's own train set. The intricacies of how it all worked were usually fascinating, but...

I gazed at a portrait on the wall, allowing the detail to overwhelm my eye. It was, admittedly, stimulating: great dark swirls of colour, executed in the style of Francis Bacon, it showed Charlotte sitting stern, imperious, upright; measuring all against her unbending standards. A difficult pose to hold for anyone, I thought.

The conversation had now moved on to the relative merits of tractors against low loaders. Why had I got involved with these relics of an age when farming and landownership dictated life for the overwhelming mass of the country? It was a pattern of behaviour and thinking utterly baffling to my city friends. My mind wandered further, out of the door, and along a lane of memory.

After a couple of seasons of being the "wee timorous beastie" at the back of the hunt, hacking along with the old ladies and avoiding the jumping bits at all costs, I had been persuaded by my mentor and friend, livery yard owner Colin, or Col to his friends, that my old Dobbin was not becoming to a man of my newfound stature and perceived means. I needed a new horse, and to get one we had to go to Ireland.

I had thus found myself one hot August bank holiday weekend with Col in County Tipperrary, staring at the horses he was evaluating for me. My technical knowledge did not extend far beyond four legs plus tail plus head equals good. It was a relief when Col was minded to agreed with the native assessment that the enormous, glossy chestnut beast standing in front of us that parched afternoon was "Just the suitin' of yer, Sir". The horse, coming into its own at five years of age, was bought, called Michael in honour of the unusually honest vendor, and ferried home. By the time the hunting season started I was the proud owner of a young, knowledgeable, and powerful horse, well suited to the challenges of the Blankshire countryside. I spent hours practising, improving what the cognoscenti called my seat, jumping things, and trying to understand the differences between my old Dobbin and this very serious tool.

Slightly awed, I continued to consciously avoid the quick jumping days in the parts of the country where the only known way from A to C was via a variety of highly dangerous Bs – "B" being BIG PLACES. My horse had moved on, but my approach to riding had not. Challenges were there to be ducked.

And then my eyes were opened.

We met at the Colonel's on a bright, chill Monday morning in November, thirty-five of us, perched on our horses, ready to enjoy the traditional hospitality of the hunting meet. The sunlight etched our shadows into the surrounds, horses clattered around the farmyard, and greetings were exchanged. Our breath billowed as the more doughty practically inhaled the whisky-cherry brandy mix this particular Colonel always offered us, known as The Percy Special, or, more colloquially, jumping juice. Taken with the fruitcake, cheese, and sausage rolls, this very respectable mid morning snack, for most of those on horseback, would also represent lunch. The dogs, or hounds as I was learning to call them, sat patiently, all thirty-seven of them, under the control of Anthony, the huntsman. Crisp and smart in his red coat and white breeches, he surveyed his temporary domain and subjects, as for the next few hours he would take precedence over all.

Without a word being spoken, Anthony picked up his horn from the saddle. There was the briefest of toots, a request of "Hounds, please", and the throng parted to permit his passage. He took his hounds, bouncing about his feet, on to the lane and towards a small wood.

One of the pedestrians, a long time foot follower and wise after forty years shook, his head at me. "Now then, 'Ector, dunno why 'e's a bothering. Them's 'aven't found in yon for twenty years since…"

Down the road the hounds went, into a hedge back, and then, against all the formbook, there was a blur of red and a bold young fox shot across the road fifty yards in front of the hounds towards the high ground – the way a fox was never supposed to go. Now what to do?

Anthony, sharp as ever, swung into action. A sharp toot of his horn, hounds askirl and aswirl at his feet, and then the beginnings of a cry as he encouraged them onwards.

"Yeeu, lads. Leu in, lads. Try, lads. Yo in there, try, try." Archaic words, thrilling words, greeted by an even more thrilling response: a muffled cry, a detection, an awareness from the hounds. "Our king is right, our leader knows. Look to 'im, lads, look to 'im. We smells 'im, we sniffs 'im, we knows 'im, we're arter 'im. 'E's been 'ere. Come, come, the chase is on. The chase is ours now, now."

Then, as these messages passed between the hounds, the group consciousness united into one, all in a second. One moment a collection of random fish, now they coalesced into a shoal; no longer working singly, they picked up and came together, threw themselves over and through the roadside hedge, and suddenly all of them were on the grass. The scent unfolding, they owned the trail from front to end; a great mobile teardrop flying across the grassy field beyond. Their cry, ragged and urgent, almost a scream, was thrilling to the senses. Horses and riders were coming alive. Michael under me was excited, snorting, pawing at the ground. He knew this craic; this was his life, his purpose. Anthony in front urged his horse on down the lane towards an imposing five bar gate and flew over it. A couple in front of me followed, leaping big and bold, and then…and then…the way to the gate was clear, open in front of me.

Of course, I did what I always did in this situation: I sat back. I heaved on the reins. WE DO NOT DO FIVE BAR GATES. Captain to engine room chief, engines full reverse, ching ching. The new chief engineer under me however, had been to a different school. He was not listening; his eyes were on a wider imperative; he ignored my hands on the reins, shook his head, and lifted himself into a trot. Now he locked on to the gate; it was clear in an instant where we were going, and this wasn't an agreement I had been a party to. What to do? What to do?

I remembered my instructor explaining in this situation it was more dangerous to try and stop the horse. One had to go with it and press the legs against its sides. "Kick on, kick on" was the instruction, and with awful clarity I remembered the signal to go, to encourage the horse. I slackened my grip, and squeezed. Michael did exactly as he'd been taught, launching from his trot into a wonderfully collected canter, square on to the gate. My heart racing and sinking, the bloody great gate in front of me, I was thinking uselessly, I DON'T DO GATES. No time to think or change. What do they say? How do I do it?

"I know," a voice from the past said, "grab the horse's neck strap, and keep off his gob." Another stride and we flew. We soared, and if the gate was nearly five foot we cleared it by another foot. A tall man, I must have been twelve or fourteen foot in the air; briefly floating, then landing. Michael, his stride uninterrupted, carried us onwards, galloping after Anthony and the hounds…

Now…now I was a Blankshire hunter. The clouds were mine to walk on as the adrenalin rushed and raced, fuzzed and agitated through my system. This was the way to live.

"Preston." I caught the word and snapped back into focus in Alex's living room. Frank was raising the latest "cause célèbre" with Alex.

"M'Lord, see, it's like this. One or two people are unhappy that your gamekeeper, Preston – yer know, young Preston? Well, he has been helping out in the hunt stables, and, a bit tricky to say this…" Frank squirmed, visibly uncomfortable, "but it's being suggested the hunt is being asked to pay 'is wages."

The situation that Frank was referring to was, in fact, a little more complex, although I guessed he was hoping for a resolution that didn't involve a blow-by-blow exposé of what was widely rumoured. I rewound the allegations in my mind. From time to time, Alex had been accustomed to sending Preston to help out in the stables, but it was now being suggested that Preston had taken a very deep and personal interest in the head girl, Cassie. It appeared his interest had been enthusiastically and intimately reciprocated, and, horror of horrors, the reciprocation was allegedly taking place in working hours.

The time spent by Preston on hunt duties, whether official or extracurricular, had been spotted in the estate office, run mercilessly by Charlotte. Preston's time, all of it, had therefore been charged to the hunt, and the source of indignation was that the Blankshire seemed to be paying for the provision of more than one sort of oats!

Lettice sat nodding with vigour, but try as she might, nought but the faintest whisper emerged. Quite whose case she was coming to aid remained unclear.

Rather than waiting for a response, Frank carried on digging, ignoring for once the golden rule of holes, namely when in one, stop digging. "Well, M'Lord, it's awkward." He might have used the expression "conflict of interest," but mercifully he was unschooled in the ways of corporate governance. "Outside help, M'Lord, and, you know, people are talking about it." I focused on the conversation, enjoying the ambiguity implicit in the expression "outside help" while Frank twisted uncomfortably in his seat. He was as brave as a lion, but taking on Alex in his lair was testing even for Frank.

"Is it, dare I ask, M'Lord, strictly necessary for this sort of carry on to, well, be carrying on? Perhaps, yer know, we can find another way of getting these extra heavy jobs, banging and so on, done in a way that doesn't involve estate staff? Not helping the reputation of the Mastership…"

His voice tailed off, and there was a silence. The off-ended party flushed: a challenge in his own home! Alex pulled himself to his feet, and at this point I became aware of a noise coming from the kitchen. For reasons known only to herself, Charlotte had lost the ability to put the pans down quietly. A cynic might have supposed she was devoting more time to listening through the door than to her pans; an unworthy thought, given her class and intimate knowledge of good manners.

"Well, Frank, I have to say I am very surprised at your remarks. You see, as a Bicester my integrity is clearly beyond reproach. No one as far as I can recall has ever sought to question the integrity of a Bicester. Simply not done. Suggesting that the estate is seeking to profit from the assistance young Preston is so willingly and enthusiastically offering is absurd. Why, chap can't do enough to lend a hand down there. Was telling me so himself only the other day, big grin on his face, clearly enjoying being useful…"

Alex's unwillingness to listen, or lack of awareness of the gossip, was touching but typically unworldly. I could see that he was embarking upon a long toil to the peak of the moral high ground, which could take some time.

Meanwhile, the rattle of the pans was growing louder, and I intervened politely.

"Surely, Alex, this is a very small matter, hardly worthy of your consideration. If any heavy lifting or carrying on is needed – you know, servicing or whatever – we, the Blankshire, should get someone in from the local town for £4 an hour and be done with it. Then no one will have the opportunity to make these unfortunate allegations."

Again there was the counter point of a pan being noisily slammed on to the Aga. My guess was that something had already boiled over, probably a temper. Silence fell as Alex resumed his seat and considered his response, unused to being challenged in this way. The silence was broken by the sound of a knife being sharpened in the kitchen.

Alex decided his march towards the peak of self-righteous indignation should continue.

"Do you not realise how much effort that we, the Bicester family, have put into supporting the Blankshire Hounds over many, many years? No, over many generations? You, Frank, have hunted with us, man and boy, for, what, fifty years? And your father before you. Have we ever not done our duty by the Blankshire Hounds?"

"M'Lord," Frank said, awkward and squirming more than ever, "I'm sorry, it's not me who began this. I just felt it better that you were aware people are expressing concern."

I was reflecting that I was probably about to witness another fine old Bicester family tradition, namely garroting the messenger, when the kitchen door flew open with a huge thump. Charlotte strode into the room, sleeves rolled, arms wet from washing dishes, and towered over her husband – and, indeed, the rest of us!

Unfortunately, I was the focus of her ire.

"Hector, you've said little so far. You're new to all of this. I heard a suggestion, caught a suggestion should I say, that there has been discussion of this family during hunting. I'd like to know exactly which people were doing the discussing, and what they were saying about this family. I know what you people talk about when you're out on your horses, and I have to tell you that if this family has been talked about I will be very very upset."

Fortunately for me, the question was purely rhetorical. The perhaps crushing truth was that I could never recall anyone discussing Charlotte.

She paused just long enough to catch her breath before plunging on. "What you were called here tonight to discuss was the appalling state not only of the hunt finances, but also the disrespectful way that the hunt treats us as a family, and to tell you all that it's about time something was done. Do you realise we provide you with stables, kennels for 120 hounds, and four, yes four, houses for the hunt servants to live in, all for a derisory peppercorn rent of £120 a year?" Hands were well and truly on her hips now, and there was a moment's silence as she took in a deep breath.

"Well I'm in charge of the estate finances now, and I tell you we have other calls on our funds. We have a young and growing family, and yet, just as the Blankshire declares itself impoverished, it seems to be forming an orderly queue to make insulting remarks about our staff. Yes, even you lot. I'm shocked. Do you realise quite how much money needs spending on the stables? You're supposed to be a man of money after all, Hector. Go on, can you tell us? Because if you can't, I will. Round numbers will do. I'm told the hunt needs to find £35,000 to make good the dilapidations in the stables of the last hundred years. Hell – pardon my language – that would buy four small houses around here. Now this money has to be found from somewhere, and found fast, otherwise you'll be looking for a new home for all the horses. So you lot are going to have to buck up your ideas, and that includes you, Alex!"

At this point a timer went off in the kitchen, and Charlotte wheeled on her heels. It was left for Alex to try and pick up the pieces, both his and ours.

"Glass of wine anyone?"

TWO

Fountain

I T WAS THE most glorious of days to be deep in the English
countryside. Following shortly after the tempestuous
meeting of the Blankshire Masters, Alex and I were with
Thomas Bradley, the newly appointed and very important
hunt chairman. Properly the fifth Earl of Melsham, Thomas
Bradley was known locally (although only behind his back
and for reasons long since forgotten) as the belted earl. To
his very few intimates, he was simply known as Sid. The
belted earl, a man privileged both by birth and intellect, was
already ruling the hunt committee with a rod of iron and
a fierce bark. He had been asked to assess the best way
to take the Blankshire hunt forward, and so he had an
appointment with us to review the decayed and parlous
state of the hunt stables.

My friend Alex, without question also privileged by
birth, sometimes seemed to feel it a curse to have been
born into a family that had always been utterly devoted
to hunting. When obliged to deal with situations like this
I felt it was his unspoken view that if he never saw horse or
hound again the duration would be about right. In short,
the hunting gene sometimes appeared to have skipped
a generation. Part of the birthright of the Bicester family,
in addition to the 20,000 acres, was the sacred covenant

of the ancestors to maintain support for the Blankshire Hounds. It is generally supposed the veneration of the ancestors is a habit only of the East, and this is true as long as we count the east of Blankshire as part of that larger globe. And so here was Alex, a man at best diffident in expressing his views, having to bear, along with all the other obligations that came with noble birth, the obligation to help the Blankshire. If ever a more ingenious curse had been devised, I suspect he had in his forty-six years failed to identify it.

On this bright summer morning, he was of necessity spending time with the belted earl, ten years his senior, because the latter claimed a brief to see the stables. In the view of Alex, the real aim of the belted earl was to have a good sneak around.

One might suppose that such men, born to the pinnacle of everything that society has to offer and having few peers in any sense, literal or otherwise, would be the very best of friends, sharing an intimacy springing from both common purpose and rarity. After all, does not a recovering alcoholic fall upon another with great joy, simply because there is so much they have in common? One would have thought so, and so, indeed, would I. In practice, being locked together by birth and position, one great estate nestling cheek by jowl against the next, they were neighbours second and competitors first in almost all respects. Destinies entwined from birth, they had an obligation to function together, to show civility, each to the other. What they did not have to do was revel in the company of the other, and they didn't!

As the interlocutor, appointed by the Blankshire hunt to mediate in all manner of affairs, a major facet of my role was to persuade the farmers and landowners of Blankshire to permit the Blankshire Hounds and the accompanying riders (the horde) to cross their land without let, hindrance or recompense. Given that many of these stolid yeomen farmers disapproved of the notion of fun as a matter of principle, it wasn't always an easy task.

Looming large amongst the landowners who needed to be kept onside were the belted earl and Alex: between them the largest landowners in the best part of the country. The mediation of the rivalry between these two peppery individuals was central to the success of the Blankshire hunt. Back then in the 1980s the hunt ban was many years in the future, but either of these two could have achieved everything desired by the hunt saboteurs purely as a result of a bad bottle of port and a sleepless night. Managing any meeting between them was a responsibility that would make a senior diplomat sweat.

It was unlikely to go well. I had heard the enmity between the two stemmed from the fact that one, the intellectually less steam powered one, was old money ("came over with the Normans" old), whereas the belted earl and his family were a relatively recent import. The latter's gene pool was still busting with energy and, on occasion, malevolence. As such, it was whispered the belted earl was practically nouveu-riche! It seemed to me the enmity rose far more from the delight the livelier of the two took in teasing his esteemed neighbour. While Alex had a sparkle, he was essentially a shy and diffident man, and, in comparison to the belted earl, in terms of intellect he was far more a Ford Cortina than an aristocratic Bentley. And, of course, the belted earl knew this. In truth, the belted earl's *Who's Who* entry ought to have included Alex baiting as one of his principle pursuits.

The meeting itself was taking place just outside the now notorious hunt stables, built in 1834 to the very highest of standards. While standards had since moved on, the stables had very definitely not. Even on this bright summer's day the faint melancholy of decay hung over them: a decay sinking even into the quietly rotting stones and the guttering clinging to its function by a few flecks of rust.

The belted earl was straight into the attack. "Hmmmm. You know, Alex, I've not been here since the days of my dear old dad. Doesn't seem to have changed much, or am I missing something?"

This was tantamount to an accusation of stables abuse. Not quite as serious as abuse involving children, but in these circles it was a serious charge nonetheless, its gravity accentuated by its truth. As the merest glance around showed the evidence was all about, from the damp creeping up the walls of the open stables to the sole means of heating: a great open fireplace sitting at the back of the main stable building. "I mean, we haven't had a coal fire in the stud up at my place for, Lawd knows, thirty years? Its like a time capsule, this place."

Alex flushed. This was not a conversation he was equipped by temperament to deal with, and his thought now was escape. It was Alex's moment to hmm, not in preparation for assault, but rather to look around for an exit. The cogs whirred, his mouth fell open, then it closed, a further grinding of rusty gears was almost audible, but no sound emerged.

The stand-off continued. Precious, agonised seconds ticked by as the brain of Alex struggled to comprehend how quickly this had begun to turn nasty. All the belted earl's superficially polite and accurate remarks were actually truly offensive, and previous encounters were clearly flashing before Alex, each containing a similar drowning man moment. Far too many episodes, I guessed.

"Of course, it will be better when..." Alex mumbled. Rather than endure further torment, he turned on his heels. His tormentor followed, scenting the molecules of hemoglobin scattered in the water. Now there was fun to be had. Alex strolled, ostensibly to a better viewing position. We turned a corner and there, behind great rusty padlocked iron gates and six foot walls, was the ruin of what had been the vegetable gardens. Now reduced to aged and blackened trees, vegetation running amok, little or no trace remained of what I imagined had once been serried rows of vegetables, soft fruit, and autumn harvest.

"Ah. So, Alex, that's to be the new site for the fountain, is it?" The belted earl was sensing an open goal. "Aiming to be just like Chatsworth House, are we? Only bigger, maybe your very own version of the Emperor Fountain, what?"

Of course, the suggestion was absurd. The gardens had not been touched for fifty years, and there was little sign the passage of another fifty would make any difference. Again the belted earl twinkled at me; he might have been a tough old boot, but his bullying humour and delicately nuanced malevolence was hard not to enjoy. As blood sports go this was unquestionably cruel, but artfully done: the strong taking advantage and devouring the weak.

Alex looked as though he had swallowed a particularly badly corked mouthful of port. Struggling for any sort of riposte to this quite extraordinary suggestion, he about faced and announced he needed to inspect the gate in the Gas Field, whatever that was, and invited us to carry on. Once Alex had gone, the belted earl took the opportunity to walk up towards the Big House, peering at the iron railings and clearly noting the level of rust.

"All a bit poor. Surprised they don't take a little more care of the place, what?" The question was clearly rhetorical. He knew exactly what he thought, and had little or no interest in the opinions of others. Ah, what a contrast all this presented to him. His acres, many thousands of them, were immaculately tended by men "wot did". "Rum way for old Alex to carry on, don't you think, what? Shall be mentioning this when I get home. Yes, really quite surprising."

We both knew it was no such thing, but this was his way of conveying his own sense of superiority, both specifically and generally. Invariably, bringing these two together was the ultimate battle; emissaries usually negotiated on their behalf, but when the two great old battleships appeared in the same stretch of sea, the stakes were high and the outcome difficult to predict. The shells they fired were of a calibre that the other recognised, and did damage; the salvos launched by their social inferiors, the cruisers and corvettes of country life, simply bounced off. As each took the views of the other very seriously, urgent intervention to stop this engagement spiralling out of control became vital.

So, how to assist Alex? The early hits from the belted earl on his exposed armour meant he was now in full retreat while making smoke.

"So, its clear to me," launched forward the belted earl, ostensibly for my benefit but more likely to give his vocal cords the benefit of further exercise, "the solution is pretty straightforward."

His solution was going to be the last thing Alex would wish to hear. If there were to be another salvo it could easily be the last straw after the early hits. I decided a little bit of heading off was required before further uncharted waters were encountered.

"Look, Thomas, sir," I was not, and never would be, one of his intimates, "Alex has a lot to think about. He is obviously worried that time is catching up with the stables. I know the estate is not prepared to do much unless the hunt looks a bit lively, so let's postpone the discussion of your suggestion until it's been properly costed. After all, Alex does need to see some progress from the hunt committee before committing the estate to further expenditure. It's hardly his fault that the hunt committee has allowed the place to get into such a state."

Reluctantly the aging peer agreed. Perhaps sensing that, for now at least, he had gone quite far enough, he decided to quit while comfortably ahead. Alex baiting for the day done, he turned on his heels and stalked away towards his car. As he made his exit, Alex returned.

"Well, tell me, what was he on about? Always got some new theory about how he can pretend to help. Seems to forget that it's my family who have made the Blankshire work for the last 250 years, and his dropped in here five minutes ago." Technically sometime in the 1890s, I understood, but no mind. Now was not the time to interrupt.

"And he, that man, d'yer know what? He's never put his hands in his pocket for anything useful yet! Well I tell you, Hector, I've had about enough of him wandering around my land, making flippant remarks."

"I'm sorry, Alex, I only think he was trying to help. You know, work out some priorities, decide what's needed to put things in a better state of repair, and it is likely the committee will be prepared to pay for it."

Alex snorted. "Just nosey parkering is what he's about." We ambled slowly away from the stables and across the deer park, the dappled late summer sunshine through the park trees beginning to dispel the memory of the visit. As we strolled, Alex's humour improved slightly.

"So, Hector, you tell me, how do we improve our finances so that the hunt can pay for all the repair work needed without that man coming on to my land again?" That man had more than enough wealth to sort all of this out without a second thought.

"Alex, the easy answer would be to get the earl to contribute. Trouble is, he is famous for many things, and one claim to fame I would never dispute is that, while his arms are short, his pockets are invariably mysteriously deep. You and I need to find a way to charm him…" I paused. The expression on Alex's face had turned decidedly bilious.

"What did yer say? We charm him? When hell freezes over!" That rarest of things from my friend: a definitive statement. Pity it was a tad on the negative side. I realised my suggestion was conspicuous more for its naïveté than its acceptability.

"Or do I find another way?" I offered limply.

"You'll find a way to get him on side? I'm sure you will, bright fellow like you. Won't be easy, mark my words. Could solve a few problems though, what?"

The hint of a wintery smile re-emerged on Alex's face, so emboldened I resumed. "Yes, well I've just got to persuade him to do the decent thing. Can't be that difficult, surely?" Here I paused, aware I was probably wandering into a mire of my own making. I hadn't the faintest idea how I would persuade the belted earl to tell me the time of day, but unfortunately, while my flight of fancy was clearly going too far, it was also being very well received. Alex was gazing at me benignly, and I caught the sight of a thought beetling slowly across his craggy brow.

After due and necessary time for reflection, he announced, "Was thinking, we've been let down by an American friend. Usually shoots with us after Christmas. January time, actually, the family day, but he's had a heart attack or something. Very inconvenient of him."

"Probably more so for him than for you," I observed.

"Well yes, maybe so, but I do have a point. Let me finish, please."

As was often the case with Alex's roundabout ways, something of value was about to be conferred, and I decided to shut up and discover what he had in mind.

"Anyway, I was wonderin', perhaps you'd like to come along instead of him? A day's shootin' with us, bit of a filler. The day probably won't be up to very much." Typical of his self-deprecation, the shooting was famously good, and an invitation like this was coveted countywide. "Of course, he'll be there," Alex continued, indicating towards the earl's tatty old car which was now pulling away from the stables, "but generally the company will be pretty good. Think you might enjoy it, and it will be a good opportunity for you to work your charm on that fella. What do you think?"

He tailed off into a ruminative silence, reminiscent of one of the bulls farmed for him up on top of the hill. Under normal circumstances this would have been an uncommonly generous offer, but clearly there was rather more to it. However, the warning signals, so obvious with hindsight, were ignored by me. In the eyes of Alex I had been elevated to new levels: potential scourge of the belted earl and champion of the noble Bicester family. Perhaps, and rather more likely, I had been elevated to the role of plain mug.

THREE

Oats

I<small>T WAS A</small> couple of days after the meeting between the two armoured leviathans of Blankshire county. The bright summer weather had continued, and it was just the sort of day to jump into the hunt pick-up and go and see some farmers. This was an occasional pleasure of mine, and it allowed me to catch up on a little local gossip, as well as ensure any misunderstandings from our winter's escapades were cleared up at leisure. Having seen half a dozen farmers over the course of the afternoon, I decided that, as I had the trailer with me, it was a perfect opportunity to venture almost on to the moor top to see my fellow Joint Master Frank – he of the facial tufts.

Frank farmed on a remote spot called Thatcher's Sedge. As I pulled up in the hunt pick-up, complete with trailer attached, he limped down from the house.

"Afternoon, Frank. How are you?"

"Well thanks, Master. Glorious day." Looking around, I took in the immensity of the views, rolling away with the smudge of the sea in the far distance.

I glanced at Frank. "Bit of fun you had with our leader at the meeting the other night, Frank. Got your point across, the rest of us thought, about right. Not an easy man to talk back to, our leader. Not used to it, that's for sure.

Outcome's a bit tricky, mind you, but it needed saying. I have to say I felt a little apprehensive, knowing Charlotte had been listening with all those knives to hand, eh Frank? And you first in the firing line. Rather thought I was about to witness a live demonstration of how to turn guts into garters!"

Frank grinned. "Well, thing is, Hector, I've known Charlotte for a lot of years, and she does rather enjoy a dramatic entrance. Very conscious of who she is – bit too much so in my view, but there'll be no changing her now. Fact is, she was wrong about young Preston. 'E shouldn't be doing what he's doing, not on our time anyway, but about the broader situation I rather agree with her. There's all those grand folk prancing around as so called Blankshire sportsman as though they own the place, and yet it's the Bicesters who seem to keep getting stuck with the bills, and that can't be right. Our sport has to be paid for, so I reckon what she said, what the Bicester family want and expect us to achieve, wants doing anyway.

"Now then, Hector, what can I do for you?"

"Frank, I've just come to pick up another installment of those oats you very kindly offered for the horses."

"Aye, those. Well the ones in the barn over yonder are the only oats you'll be getting around here, I'm afraid, but you're very welcome to them. As long as you load them yourself, of course." He grinned again. "Mind you, you've come on a good day. It's my birthday. There's not a lot to celebrate around here, but we do like to do birthdays proper. First, however, you'll find some empty oat sacks over by the hopper. By the time you've finished filling those I should have sorted the new sheep out and we'll both be ready for a drink, so do pop into the house. It's only once a year I celebrate me birthday!"

I took the hunt trailer round the corner, and after forty

minutes of shifting, sweating, and swearing, I had a trailer full of moor grown oats. I walked into the kitchen, which was modern, clean, tidy and warm, but not characterful it must be said. However, with the characters that lived in it, it didn't need to be. I had grabbed a bottle of whisky from the back of the pick-up, but as soon as Frank saw it he waved it away.

"You won't be needin' that here. It's my birthday and my house, so it's my hospitality. Come, sit yourself down, lad."

Leaving my bottle and my boots by the door, we settled down with a bottle of Mr Bell's finest Scotch, straight but for a drop of local spring water – no mains water up on this remote spot.

"So, Frank, we seem to have put a stop to young Preston getting his leg over at our expense, and that's got to be an improvement. Interesting, I spent most of yesterday morning wandering around the stables with Alex and the belted earl. It was a fascinating experience. Talk about oil and water. I thought Alex was going to explode. He couldn't get rid of the old boy fast enough, while the belted earl seemed determined to be rude about every aspect of the estate. Five more minutes and I would have been expecting pistols at dawn. Has it always been like this?"

Frank took a sip of his whisky. It might be his birthday, but there was little sign of him overdoing anything. That was not his way.

"Known the belted earl almost as long as I can remember. Always been a distant sort of fella. Now his father, there was a grand man, and a good one too. Thought nothing of visiting a farmer if there had been a problem during a huntin' day, bottle of whisky at the ready. Well, it's a bit of a story this. Not for general circulation, don't want people thinking I'm soft."

That was unlikely, I caught myself thinking.

"Anyway, ten years ago, so as you know, I caught my leg in the damn combine. It was a bit of a mess. Hurt too. Anyway, seven long weeks I was in hospital. Bloody hell, it was miserable. Full of ill people. By the time I got out, in a wheelchair, I really thought I'd never sit on a horse again. 'Lucky to be alive,' they said. Obviously I was a bit down about the whole thing, and told Sue and the kids what the doctors had explained. I said to the family they'd best sort through my huntin' things, and sling out or sell anything they didn't want. It seemed like the right thing to do. Normally my red hunting coat was hung up in sight in the kitchen, and when I first came home it felt as though it were taunting me. Got so I couldn't stand the sight of it.

"Then, it vanished. Thought nothing of it – glad it was gone, if the truth be told.

Things improved, quicker and better than anyone expected. By early December I was beginning to walk, and considering getting going on a horse again." Frank rapped his foot with his glass: it rang out with a hollow clonk. "I was getting used to using this bloody strange artificial thing by then. By the middle of December I had decided that was it: I'd be fit to go hunting soon. Wasn't sure when, but the next step was to find me things. So I tried, quietly of course, looking for them, and mostly they came to light – breeches, boots, and so on – scattered in different places about the house. Hidden away I reckon, but I didn't like to ask Sue direct. Didn't want her to know I was planning to ignore the doc's advice. When I hinted about my coat – you know, like 'What have you done with it? Did you get a fair price?' she was bloomin' vague. Wasn't sure where my red coat was, and anyway I wouldn't be needing it again, so why was I so keen to find it? That question left me a bit stumped!"

Frank clonked his foot again and grimaced at his own silly pun.

"I asked son James to nip up to the attic to have a look for it, but he just got shifty and referred me back to HQ. Pretty slippery he was too, looking back. Do you know what had happened? The whole family knows what I'm like: that I'd be getting back on a horse again if humanly possible. Sue had seen old man belted earl out hunting and told him I was on the mend, so he'd volunteered for one of his men to come over when I was out. They'd taken my red coat! Sue had dug it out for them, of course. So the reason I couldn't find the damn thing was because my own wife had arranged for it to be stolen, and by 'im!

"But there was method in the madness. I came down on Christmas morning, and there it was. All my hunt kit laid out, complete with the red coat. And this is the bit: bright, new, shiny gold Blankshire Hunt buttons sewn on to it. Turns out old man belted earl had personally sewn on 'is own special hunt buttons. Proper nine carat gold ones. Amazing things, never tarnish, never need cleaning, fourteen of them in all. Normally only he and the hunt staff wear 'em. He had slipped the red coat back on Christmas Eve when he knew I'd be out sorting the sheep down at the market, which meant it was all laid out, specially like. Of course, I knew where the buttons had come from straight away. Only he had anything that smart. My whole damn family had been in on the conspiracy. I have to say, well, I pretended to be cross, but actually I was so surprised I couldn't keep it up for very long. Have to admit I was slightly touched. Apparently, the old earl had said it was worth doing if it helped get me back on a horse again."

Frank paused, a certain dampness around the eyes suggesting he had been more than slightly touched. We sat quietly for a few moments, then he continued.

"The gesture made me even more determined to get back on a horse and on with my life. Meant a right lot.

Appreciation, bit of recognition, does you good. You know you belong, don't you?"

He sipped at his whisky again; a big swallow intended, I suspected, to cover his own surprise at having shown a little of his feelings.

"Now, the old M'Lord passed on soon after that. The young 'un, he's a different kettle of fish. Picture of rectitude. Never knowingly been on the wrong side of an argument. That's him, at least in his opinion. Very bright, but very much focused on the sound of his own voice and the cleverness of his mind. There's nobody he would rather listen to than 'imself, yer might just have noticed."

"Yes, that's rather my impression of him, although I hardly know him at all. He was very keen to 'goose' poor old Alex. Almost cruel, really. Thing is, if we are to raise some serious money we will need his support. Bit awkward for me, you see, because I rather rashly volunteered to lead the charge. I'm realising that was the easy bit, as I'm stuck now as to what comes next. What is pretty obvious, though, is that getting him on side is utterly crucial. Any thoughts?"

"It's a tricky one. I'm tempted to say 'When you find out, let me know, can't you?' We've all had a go, one way or another. I've got no feeling for him, what he's about or what floats his boat. The only thing he and his dad have in common is they have both been pretty reckless, although in different ways. His father was the devil to follow across country. God, we had some days when I was but a lad. Fast on a 'oss – no holding him when his blood was up. Money no object when it came to the horses in his stables, I can tell you, and he was pretty reckless in other ways too. Old boy could be a bit naughty, he installed his mistress in a house in the park of the Big House. Gardener's Cottage it was, and, well, you can imagine the fun the wags had with that arrangement."

We both sipped, and reflected upon the possibilities. Sue appeared and broke the silence by asking if I wished to stay for supper.

"Thanks, Sue. Another time, but after this I need to be on my way."

Frank continued, now talking of the present belted earl.

"Well, as I say, although he always comes across as very cold, proper and analytical, actually..." Here Frank, although in his own kitchen, looked around surreptitiously. Very discreet, our Frank. "Actually, he is a rather enthusiastic gambler on the side, so I hear. I gather he's not above a certain amount of gerrymandering – yer know, playing around. Nothing ever proved, of course, but a story I heard." He leaned in to me, whisky glass cupped between his hands and chin.

"He has a few point to point horses. Amateur things. Local race meetings. One time, some Jockey Club officials turned up and wanted to check his horses. The Jockey Club runs racing, as yer know, always on the look out for cunning stunts. They wanted to make sure that the lightning fast running machine that had just won the Blankshire point to point by ten lengths was the same three legged donkey that had either pulled up or finished last in its seven previous outings. Blow me, but it appeared the knacker man had been half an hour earlier and taken said nag on its final ride to the glue factory. Anyway, so the story goes, there were an awful lot of red faces up at the stud.

"I reckon some pretty hurried thinking took place. Quick explanation was the order of the day. 'Terribly sorry, Mr Jockey Club. Horse is gone. No possibility we would have swapped horses at the last moment. What, we employees of Lord Belted Earl? No, we don't know which knacker man.' Nothing was ever said, of course, but it makes you think. Bit more to that than a coincidence, I'd have said. Talked about a lot, but nothing ever proved. It's not as though he needed the money, anyway, so it's probably just a rumour. Well, you can just imagine it!"

Another sip of whisky. "But I'll tell you this, 'Ector, what I do know for sure is the belted earl loves a wager. Puts a gleam in his eyes, especially if he thinks he's going to win. I've been a tenant of his family all my life, but we don't see anything much of him, other than on a hunting day. He rolls around the lanes in that old Lancia of his. Knackered, that car – I wouldn't let my seventeen year old drive something as shabby as that. He follows on for a while, and then gets tucked into that big picnic hamper he always carries in the back. And also, from what I can see into the port. Best steer clear of him if you see him much after two o'clock, as his steering can be a bit erratic. Not so good on his pins, either. Inclined to sway a bit when he gets out of the car to dish out his orders, take that as a tip from me."

This seemed like a good cue to get on my way. Although normally the most reticent of men, once Frank had started talking it was sometimes difficult to staunch the flow. However, in all his gossip about the belted earl there was something of value. I was now on familiar territory: understanding the eternal battle between fear and greed was what I'd been doing for twenty years and using it to my advantage. I was beginning to feel this world wasn't so strange after all.

FOUR

Gin

I WOKE THE following morning with a growing sense of another fine mess I had got me into. I had to find £35,000 to save the stables, and while I had enjoyed a fair degree of success in the city, I was not, under any circumstances, about to become the one man Bank of the Blankshire hunt. Clearly I could use the help of Alex, but the belted earl, the wealthiest man in Blankshire, was, for now, off limits. And yet, he was the one sure route to salvation. At a stroke from his pen, Jack, or least this relatively impecunious master of foxhounds, could be free! It was clear that the earl must be dragged at some stage, if necessary kicking and screaming, into the arena to play his birth anointed role. While there was no love lost between the earl and Alex, their actions set the tone for the whole of the Blankshire landed set. At least I now had some insights as to the earl's pressure points, and very useful these sort of insights had been to me over the years. They gave me a card or two to play with.

There matters rested until a couple of weeks later. We had been out with the horses conducting the strange ritual that signals the start of the hunting season, known as Autumn hunting, which for reasons of utter obscurity is initiated just as dawn cracks. As always in September, we had met at 6am at the most ridiculous of places. Pilgars

Farm, perched high above the sea, could only be reached by dragging our horse boxes up an unmade track on a one in three hill. This added twenty minutes to the journey, but we were wanted there by old Bill Hebron. As he loved to tell us, hounds had been visiting since 1909 when he was "nobut a bairn" (I supposed he meant child), and he was, as always, delighted to see us again.

Not only was old Bill Hebron delighted to see us, but so was the wind, which howled its greeting at us, and so was the cold face numbing rain. We climbed on to our horses and made for the lee of the barn. Here the gathered few, a dozen or so, had time to contemplate the icy grey vastness of the sea, rolling away into the distance, the grey waters offset by the white caps of the waves. Truly a marvellous day, but only for those lucky enough to be still tucked up in bed.

However, one of the pleasures of the day was that Mrs Dobinson was out. Lucinda Dobinson, or Lucy to her friends, was in her early sixties, and was a stalwart of all things Blankshire. As our slow day of exercising our hounds passed, and my extremities got steadily colder and colder, we chatted. The icy rain seemed to regard its attack on us as personal and redoubled its effort, and I began to really regret my lack of gloves. It was clear Lucy had also endured enough.

"Hector, it's nearly ten o'clock now. I insist you and I knock off early. This is ridiculous, I've seen less blue at a Conservative party conference than on you. Even your nose is turning blue, a most unedifying sight if you don't mind me saying, and it's very unhelpful to let body parts fall off, dear boy. You've only just started in this job, and we need to take care of you. I know just the reviver you need." I have to say the suggestion was very attractive. Half an hour in front of the Aga might bring my newly blued extremities back to life, and as an added bonus she and her husband, Nick were well known for their hospitality and culinary skills. Things were looking up.

It was a huge relief to shut the back door of the Dobinson's farmhouse firmly on the gale, which continued to howl its alarming easterly tales of Siberian winters. We passed through a boot room and scullery into a large kitchen, scruffy and rather tatty. The Aga in the corner, like its owner, showed much evidence of its age. However, notwithstanding the passage of time, the kitchen, with great picture windows looking out on to an immaculate garden, was an immensely cheerful place. Everything was exactly as it should be: the big, old wooden table in the centre of the room on the red quarry tiles; the dogs heaped waffling and whiffling quietly in their baskets.

"Now then, young Master Hector," boomed Nick, who had been waiting, I suspect, with anticipation for what came next, "we always enjoy one drink after autumn hunting and before breakfast, although I know it's ever so slightly naughty." A conspiratorial grin and a wink followed, as I stood, rendered numb and speechless by the cold. A bottle of Bombay Sapphire gin appeared, and within seconds almost half of it had been slopped into three huge glasses. These were topped up with a large measure of Stone's Original green ginger wine, and the faintest splash of tonic water.

Nick fell onto his glass with unbridled enthusiasm. "This'll sort you out, mark my words." I gulped at the unusual concoction, then coughed and spluttered. This was kill or cure time.

It's difficult to describe the sensation of drinking a gin cocktail at 11am. Somehow it's different: naughtier and nicer, the harshness of the spirit catching at the throat. No doubt about one thing: it was pretty good antifreeze. The blood was slowly and painfully returning to my extremities. As I thawed we began to talk, and the feeling of slight drunkenness led the conversation into areas that otherwise would not have been reached.

"So then, young Hector, tell us about your love life." Nick's willingness to round my age down by twenty or so years was always enjoyable, even if it was a rather too obvious piece of flattery. Who cared? He was a very nice man being thoroughly charming, and in my slightly inebriated state it felt pretty good. Lucy then interrupted her husband's particularly leading question by placing in front of us the most colossal English breakfast; if the gin didn't get me, the cardiac arrest surely would!

However, after the bone-numbing cold of the early morning it tasted good, super life-saving superlatively good. Hot buttered toast; free range fried eggs, runny and bright yellow; black pudding, slightly shrivelled and cooked just so; succulent, fat-oozing sausages; fried bread glistening on the plate. My manners slightly deserted me as the craving for substantial, sustaining, fleshy protein needed to be satiated. I ate, and I ate. Nick munched in companionable silence, but Lucy's conversation was not to be interrupted.

"Well, Nick, aren't you going to ask him how they are going to solve the financial crisis? I'm told by the belted earl that the stables are in a terrible state, and he has made it quite clear he is not going to lift a finger to help, wicked old man," she muttered, more to herself than anyone else.

Nick simply said, "A gentleman doesn't talk over breakfast," and resumed his munching. The silence fell again, broken only by the scampering of the terriers who didn't believe humans deserved a hundred percent share of the good things placed tantalisingly out of their reach. Once Lucy had cleared her plate and attended to the washing up, helped by me (but not Nick, who was polishing his plate with an oversized piece of bread), she began to prepare lunch. God, they can eat, I thought to myself, and then the idea hit me: one thing that seemed to accompany every aspect of Blankshire country life was the consumption of really good grub. How did they do it? What was it they cooked? Could they be persuaded to share their secrets? All of them had their own idiosyncratic approach to cooking, and so it was conceived: the embryonic Blankshire Cookbook!

"Lucy," I ventured, "do you suppose, if I were to ask nicely, you would be kind enough to give me your recipe for your homemade black pudding? And what if we were to ask Kate Ward for her Star Gazey pie? Because, you know, we could combine all these things into one place..." I explained, and the idea was launched. Would it gain a life?

Lucy chewed meditatively on a piece of toast. "Yes, mmm, yes. I could ask Mrs Hall, the old colonel's widow, about her lemon drizzle. Always wondered how she did that, and don't want it going to the grave with her..." So now the embryonic idea, a mere scrap of frogspawn seconds ago, was splitting and dividing while remaining whole.

"And then how about so and so? And old Sir N up at the Hall? He's as queer as a coot, you know, but all his boyfriends end up getting really quite chubby. Sure he'd be delighted to tell us a little of how he does it. And then, and then, why don't I illustrate it? And I can dig out some pictures from the olden days. The Bicesters and the belted earls of this world, why, I'm sure they will have some fascinating pictures from before the war. And we can get that wonderful hunting journalist, Pomponious Ego, to write us a foreword – if he can get over himself, of course. But I can usually manage that – he's a third cousin on my mother's side."

In the manner of a Formula One racing driver, we had gone from a standing start to flat out in no time, and all it had taken was one small but intriguing idea, mixed with half a pint of gin, and a lady whose creativity simply needed an outlet. The fight to find the funds had begun.

FIVE

A Party Planner?

A ND THEN CAME the work. Here my alliance, sealed in gin with Lucy, came into play. By this I mean her formidable connections were wheeled into action. This meant a lot of work for her, a newsletter written by me, telephone lines humming, and everyone desperate for their own favourite recipe to be included. We talked at length on the phone, discussing the right printer, who could find suitable photos, whether or not the thing should be in full colour, the size of the print run, and so on, and on. I quickly became aware that between us we had an operating mind and a guiding consciousness, and they weren't, in truth, mine. Lucy was supplying the dynamism behind the project. I was simply a sounding board.

It all began to come together in record time, but not without complications.

The hunt had met at the small village of Pinch-Me-Near-Forest, a curious medieval name I believe. The wood just outside the village, known as Pogle's Wood, was a beautiful, wild, overgrown place, thick with wildlife. Annoyingly we were not able to take the hounds there; its owner, a rotund former hunting lady, had banned the hunt indefinitely after catching her husband up to no good with another member of the Blank shire Hunt. Overnight, she became the only really

46

impassioned 'anti' in the county, loathing with a fiercely articulated passion (ranting was another term) everything she had previously professed to adore. Therefore we had to skirt past her land before getting on with the job in hand. As we rode down the lane that flanked Pogle's Wood, I thought what a marvellous nature reserve it might one day make, if the buying of it could be found. An idea for another day, but just the sort of challenge I'd enjoy.

As we reached "our" territory, Lucy trotted up to me, an expression of grim determination on her features. "You do realise, Griffiths, that this is the last time I'll do anything for you bloody lot, don't you?"

At that moment there was a shout and a holler in the distance, and a great cry went up as the hounds appeared, brown and white specks on the far side of the small wood. In front of them, an orange tail shot away. The chase was on.

"Look lively, Lucy. Let's talk about it later." Michael, my horse, was on his tipity toes; he was in his seventh season, and he knew (at least, he thought he knew) far more about the job than I did. He began a slow jog on the spot, while the sound of the full pack discovering the fresh scent created a rapture of hound music, spine tingling and urgent. Michael knew exactly what it meant, and was desperate to follow. Then came the signal, and he launched himself into the briefest of trots, then canter, and then charged across the grass of the field in a full gallop. I stood up in the stirrups so he could move freely, leaning forward, the wind across my face and the glorious smell of England in my nose.

We came to a brook. Horses and hounds checked briefly, pausing as the scent vanished, then splashed through it and moved on. Ahead of me was Lucy, she and her horse moving like greased lightning, so whatever had upset her was to be a mystery for a little longer. Suddenly the scent vanished again, and as abruptly as the commotion had started it ended. The hounds casted around; their customer had given them the slip!

Lucy was nearby now.

"Lucy, sorry, but in all the tumult I rather thought I heard you suggest you were less than happy."

"Now then, dear boy," she had a remarkably steely glare when she chose "you know I have done a lot of work on your little book?"

"I do."

"And have I asked a lot of you?"

"Well, no. I'd say you've been very patient with my lack of expertise."

"Well of course I have, you silly boy, no need to snivel." I wasn't, but I saw her point. Clearly I had missed something fairly major.

"Let me explain it to you in simple language. The deal, which, incidentally, I thought a man of your intellect would have worked out, is that I do the donkey work, and you" here she pointed at me with her hunting whip, beady eye squinting down it "arrange to make sure it sells. Now what that means, I'd have thought, is that we require a Party, with a capital P, and it must be in a Big House. There must be fountains of champagne, delicious nibbles, perhaps a small orchestra. Everyone will come, enjoy themselves immensely, then depart creaking under the weight of their brand new cook books. Of course, I could ask around and arrange it myself, but as you know I've done rather a lot already, and a request from a Blankshire Master carries far more consequence. Really, I'd have thought you'd have known all of this. It's how we do things. For an intelligent man, you can be remarkably stupid."

Seeing my discomfort she patted me on the knee, gave me an all forgiving grin, and moved off in the direction of the circling hounds, leaving me to think and puzzle. Perhaps a sign on my back: "Broad shoulders, all crosses borne stoically" was needed, as this was certainly how it felt.

In solving one problem by creating a cookbook, I had generated another: how to maximise its sales. Typically, Lucy was way ahead of me. Another skill, Party-with-a-capital-P organiser, needed to be added to my list of attributes. At that moment I felt rather hapless.

The good thing about a day out hunting is there's seldom too much time for introspection. The activity generates for too many external inputs, the need to stay upright on half of ton of horse flesh for one. I switched my attention away from self pity and on to the hounds, who were casting around, thinking, puzzling, and trying to work out what to do next.

There was a whimper. An old, experienced hound, Frogman, had scented something and was sharing his insight with the others. A few hounds looked over to him, then suddenly, without an explanation, half a dozen began to tell the tale. They had found the sniff too: the scent they were looking for. Like me, they had been put right. They were now correct, and they broadcast their news to one another.

Like them, a period of thought and reflection, of casting around for the right approach, had been necessary for me. The new challenge, the Party organisation, needed thought. Not now, but later. Michael brought me sharply back into the present with a small buck. The circus was moving on, and he was not about to let us be left behind.

SIX

A Venue

TIME PASSED. I sat at home, reflecting on next steps.
Recipes had been contributed from all and sundry; the
foreword had been written; the book was coming together
beautifully, but the question of the launch party needed
urgent resolution. So far I had discussed various solutions
at considerable length with myself; sadly, this seemed to be
a particularly ineffective method of finding a venue. My
telepathic powers were failing me yet again. There was no
doubt about it: I was going to have to talk to people. But
to whom? And where to next? After all, even a county as
sprawling as Blankshire only had so many Big Houses, and
so many individuals who supported us.

The answer, I decided, was to go and see William, a land-
owner in his early forties. Inevitably, he was from a long line
of Williams who had the joy of owning a small but perfectly
formed Big House. As I walked into the entrance hall of Chez
William, I enjoyed the black and white tiles on the floor, dramatic oil paintings of great yachts the ancestors had owned,
a long dining table to seat thirty and, naturally, a large bath in
the corner. The origin of the bath and its position in the hall
was the subject of some debate. The most likely version was
that a misheard instruction to a builder had led to it being
removed from its original home upstairs, but the journey to

the tip had ceased in the hall. It remained there to this day, unconnected to either water or drains, an occasional bed for the labradors, a playhouse for William's three girls, and a talking point for every visitor.

William was good looking in a burly, well-bred sort of way, and dressed in a fashion that was uniquely him. He deserved to own the copyright of "shabby chic", dressed now in cords that had seen better days, and pullover and check shirt that were both beginning to fray. Although he appeared charmingly disarming, I had come to appreciate he was very, very sharp, as I was about to be reminded.

We sat in the kitchen. Recently refurbished, it was a delightful and sunny room, very much like its owner.

I explained about the project at some length. "And I was thinking, wondering really, do you have any thoughts on where it might be possible to hold a launch party? You know: champagne, delicious nibbles, couple of good speeches, perhaps a little orchestra, warm words and big sales all round." Not at all sure of my reception, I was talking too much; babbling, even.

"As you know, William...problems with the stables... holes in the roof...lot of money needed...every little helps..."

William suddenly interjected, "The belted earl offered to help at all?"

"Well, no, if I was to be really honest. Funnily enough, he doesn't seem at all inclined to share his, or indeed any, part of the burden."

"Hmmmm, yup." William lapsed back into silence. I glanced at William; he looked blank, his mind clearly elsewhere, then added, "What was that you said? Party here?" I hadn't said this, but it sounded encouraging.

"Well thing is, William, it had occurred to me only the other day you'd be the ideal person. Park here's a perfect setting, and this house would be brilliant for such a thing.

'Course, we'll do all the work, make sure all is left as we found it, you see?" I got all earnest and serious, trying to remember how a salesmen closes a sale. Blathering now, I thought the puzzled expression on William's face actually showed a gulf of comprehension.

"Are you sure about this party idea?"

"How do you mean? Of course I'm sure. Party here would be a marvellous idea. Very pleased I thought of it, actually." I grinned, but internally I was quailing. What could he not understand? Was he going to say no? Now that would be humiliating.

"Well, you know," he said, archly, "you said you were thinking of it, the party, only the other day and all. It's curious."

"Why?"

"Well, I was talking to Lucy a couple of weeks ago, as I do, and she told me, as only Lucy can – more a force of nature, I always think, and I tend to become the moveable object when she's around. Pretty irresistible, in an appropriate way, of course." A hint of a smile – Lucy was a good twenty years older than William. "Anyway, she laid it all out for me, just as you've done. The party, the champagne, the delicious nibbles, the small orchestra, people having a good time, all walking away with armfuls of books."

My earlier words and glorious claims to invention sounded a little hollow.

"So I was just wondering, well, obviously you both thought of it independently?" He smiled at me in a gentle, knowing way, point perhaps made. The enterprise was clearly bigger than me. Why had I ever thought otherwise?

"Well, of course you can have the party here. I've known about this for weeks," he confided. "Lucy told me all about it. If that's what the Blankshire needs, and it's what you and Lucy want, we are only too pleased to help. You give me a date and consider it done. It'll be good to have the old house full of people, it's what it was made for. I'll even throw in a crate of champagne, make sure it all goes off with a bang. Have to kick things off properly when you're a host, after all. It's the way we do things here – most of us, leastways."

Was I to be elated, irritated, or just pleased things were working? The latter seemed the best course. I sensed in a curious way that I had been tested, and had passed. Now to make it happen.

I was starting to have an uneasy feeling that it all seemed to be too easy.

SEVEN

Racquets

THE DATE FOR the Party-with-a-capital-P was set, or at least I thought it was, for early November. It was to be the first Tuesday in the month. William approved, Lucy was happy, and who else could possibly lay claim to "our" day?

I was a simpler creature in those days. Yet another Blankshire elephant trap already lay in wait, but fortunately I stumbled into it sooner rather than later. As with any hunt, the Blankshire relied upon a network of individuals who volunteered their time, and often their skills. Without exception, this was a labour of love, although the atmosphere in which it was given might not always have been seen as very loving. I have heard the complexity of the network compared to the workings of a Swiss watch, which is fine as far as it goes, but I don't recall the different parts of a Swiss watch nurturing grudges against each other, some going back more than twenty years.

The Blankshire was a little unusual at that time because it was still well supported by the great and the good of the county. The ladies of this particular set, while invariably the epitome of charm and good manners on the surface, were not to be taken for granted. Their cooperation was given enthusiastically, but on their terms, and at this stage it's fair to say my appreciation of this was not as fully developed as it was later to become.

We were out hunting at Glum's Farm, a small part of a larger estate owned by my fellow Master, Lettice, and her husband Malcolm. In addition to her occasionally withering vocal gifts (now her voice had recovered), Lettice was an organisational supremo. If I was ever engaged to start a small war, Lettice would be the head of my general staff.

Today she was mounted on her very smart cob called Toby. I always enjoyed chattering to her; her idiosyncratic sense of humour and unique insights gave a fresh twist to most things. I mentioned the book, of which she was aware, and the idea of the Party, of which she approved, and I confidently expected her to volunteer her services as a matter of course. However, as soon as I mentioned the date her face assumed a scowl, and my plan suddenly lost its wheels. "But Hector! What are you thinking of? That's a Tuesday, isn't it?"

"Well yes, it is. We're just about to print the invites."

"I'm sorry, you'll just have to change the date. You see, once a fortnight the Blankshire Ladies' Racquets Club meets. Always on a Tuesday, everyone knows that, and that's our Tuesday."

Demonstrably, not everyone did know this, but I was now lost for words. From the little I knew of the game of racquets, it was an older, faster version of squash, and that the ladies who lunched played was news to me. Lettice pressed on, which was lucky as I was still computing the images of these genteel and not so young, or slim, ladies playing racquets.

"You see over there?" She indicated a building close to the Big House which I had assumed was an old outbuilding. Apparently it was not just any old outbuilding. "There! Yes, that one. My great uncle Bertie built a racquets court back in the 1890s, when nasty games like tennis and squash had not yet developed, and myself and..." here she reeled off the names of the eight most redoubtable ladies in the Blankshire country "come to play. We are quite set in our routine. Moving the date? Pah, simply not possible. Sorry." She gave a resigned and thoroughly unhelpful shrug.

Each lady member of the racquets club was individually formidable; collectively I'd struggle to find the appropriate noun. The word "coven" sprang to mind, but before I had even given it real thought it became clear that coming between the ladies' club and its bi-monthly appointment with the racquets court was not to be undertaken lightly. Indeed, it wasn't realistically to be undertaken at all.

Lettice reiterated, in terms suitable for a class of four year olds, "Look, Hector, it's very simple. That Tuesday is no good. You'll just have change it – the date, I mean. All good otherwise. Sure it will be a huge success anyway. Carry on."

Bugger!

Yet again, I was learning that Blankshire people were not big on conciliation or compromise. Lettice, having delivered her bombshell with apparently no awareness of the egocentricity of her approach, shot off to go and see the hounds. Galileo's views about the earth revolving around the sun were feeling more and more theoretical by the moment; it was very clear that all sorts of previously unknown gravitational phenomenon were affecting my orbit. What to do next?

Full of trepidation, I called to see William. I needed advice from an expert, but his reaction was not quite what I'd expected. Instead of cursing and swearing at the sheer bloody mindedness of one or two ladies, he took it completely in his stride.

"Yes, I see. Of course, silly of me to forget. Yes, they do meet at Lettice's every other Tuesday. Have done since forever. I don't think they play very hard. They're all a bit past it now, if you know what I mean, but it's an opportunity for them to get a bit of exercise. Keeps the old building going, raises some money for the hunt, and, après racquets, they can put a reputation or two to the sword as the mood takes 'em. They make those old dears who used to sit under the guillotine knitting – yer know, the tricoteuse – seem the very soul of compassion and humanity. The Ladies' Racquets Club, Christ, even the belted earl shies clear of that lot. My old pa fell out with them once. Years before they would come for supper again. Only thing for it, as always, we will have to revolve around them. Let's go for the Thursday instead. Bit of a pain, but better only to fight the battles we can win, eh? Who says this is a paternalistic society with those matriarchs on permanent war footing? Deep waters, Hector, deep waters." He grinned at me. "Think you handled that pretty well, considering it's your first intro to 'em."

So, with another involuntary chapter of my education into the ways of the Blankshire movers and shakers complete, and a little bump in the road dealt with by waving the white flag, I went to see Lucy. I found her sitting in her kitchen, wreathed in smoke, surrounded by printers' proofs and snoozing terriers.

"Let's just have a quick read through, shall we?" At Lucy's invitation I flicked through the rough proofs.

"Lucy, this is marvellous. It looks terrific. These sketches and photos –tremendous!"

Lucy beamed. The sketches were good, and so were the variety of hunting photographs from the olden days. Various people had braved cellars and attics, and pictures from times in the past had appeared: young men looking remarkably smug, standing on the steps of Big Houses garbed in their distinctive clothing, universally wearing expressions saying "All mine, for as far as the eye can see." Other pictures showed esteemed ancestors jumping improbably large hedges. How the cameraman had known to stand just in the right spot as the horse came thundering by is anybody's guess, but the pictures unquestionably gave the book a tremendous amount of charm, as well as allowing the ancestors one last run.

As I flicked idly through what was close to being the final version, I stopped half way down a page. Just after the recipe for sticky toffee pudding was the following:

"You are a free bird.

The most I can ever hope for

Is you fly down into my garden,

Into my tree, and sing sing sing,

But only for me."

"Lucy, I don't recall us discussing the addition of, I struggled to articulate the word, but fortunately I kept my wits, ignoring its total inappropriateness: "poetry."

Just for once, Lucy blushed. "Do you like it? I've put a few in, just like it. You know, the nice things in life. We need to look inwards, take stock of our inner human and celebrate happy moments too." Reading the result of Lucy getting in touch with her inner self was making me feel slightly nauseous. This was a test of my tact.

"Lucy, this is only a personal opinion." My brain whirred, then inspiration struck. "As I recall we all agreed this was to be a cookbook, and I'm ever so slightly surprised it's become an outlet for your undoubtedly sensitive poetic soul. I'm inclined to think you ought to carry out a little cull, then we can look at all your, eermm, works together, and see if we can find another way of exposing your gifts to the world."

Just for once, the immovable object volunteered to shift, if only a few inches.

"Well, Master, if you're really sure? You do like my

work, don't you?" The sight of Lucy fluttering at me is not something I wish to dwell on. In her day she would have been a curvy lady, but sadly the curves had rather run together. The whole had rather become greater than the sum.

"Well yes, of course I like your work, but if we allow too much limelight to shine on your solo literary efforts in what, after all, is supposed to be a combined endeavour, it might be seen as you hogging the limelight. I don't think that can be right, do you?"

This approach clearly reminded Lucy of the importance of being self-effacing.

"Yes, sadly you're probably right. I was rather looking forward...no, right you are. I just thought it was an opportunity..." She tailed off, every inch the disappointed poetess, while in my head I could hear a particularly large tank clanking slowly off my lawn.

The curious thing about this episode was that, having asserted myself a little for once, things began to flow. The invitations were sent, the catering agreed and arranged with lots of willing helpers, the responses flooded back, and all of a sudden we had the beginnings of a great success. Two hundred people said "Yes", with even more likely to arrive on the evening. There was even talk of moving the bath, but that was quickly quashed by William.

"Been there too long now, got used to it. It'll have to stay. Anyway, the dogs like it."

So, finally we were set.

EIGHT

The Sour Note

THE LUXURIOUS THING about organising a party in a Big
House is that a party is exactly what a Big House is
made for. Most of the year the vast quantity of internal
space sits quiet and dormant; dust flecking in the sunshine;
dust gathering and falling in the moonlight. However, all
that space, which often prompts the modern eye to say,
"God, who'd want to live in a place this size?" suddenly
comes into its own.

I had stood and watched as food, drink, crates, car-
tons, cook books and cut flowers, prepared by the Ladies'
Racquets Club, were carried by a variety of people into the
Big House. Up the steps, past the bath which had finally
discovered a purpose: filled with ice it made the perfect
ice bucket for sixty bottles of champagne, and on to their
designated places.

The kitchen had swallowed the food. Extra tables had
been prepared, and the existing tables in the downstairs
rooms were laid with all the necessities for a proper do.
Inevitably, once the date had been sorted to their satisfaction,
the faux horror of the Ladies' Racquets Club at not being
properly consulted had transformed into an orderly queue
of highly proficient and skilled helpers, all willing to do their
bit. Lettice cooked up her homemade mushroom soup, and

very good it looked too. Rumour had it that on one occasion magic mushrooms had inadvertently been gathered for the soup by the gardener. The folk memory suggested those who had tasted it had enjoyed a very particular evening. The ravishingly rich beef casserole, a speciality of Lady Jane Belted Earl, was also to be appreciated. It had been known to convert vegans to the joys of living as carnivores, dripping gravy from their greedily overfilled mouths, such was the richness of its aroma. Others had contributed a wonderful spread of what I can only describe as proper English food: cakes and puddings, and even a huge sherry trifle.

And while the food and drink kept coming, unlike in the modern domestic home, there was no clutter. There was space for everything, and everything had space.

We had invited over 400 people, and it was pretty clear at least half were going to turn up. Probably a few more; in its own little way this had turned into one of the social highlights of the year.

William spotted me. "Ah, guest of honour. Organising supremo and organisational genius." He enjoyed overdoing his words, did our William. Flattery was inexpensive and very effective, and that, I realised, was his approach. To be honest, I was rather enjoying the build up to my little night of glory. I'd had the idea, put in a fair bit of work, and it was rather fun to be king for a day.

It was a jacket and tie sort of evening. I was wearing my very best Savile Row suit and my polishiest of shoes. The ladies of the racquets club were fussing around, all squeezed into proper tweedy skirts, with ruffles, pearls, and freshly permed hair. Tonight would give them chattering material for some months to come. William had made a supreme effort and appeared in a suit that seemed to be without holes, although I suspected the pullover he insisted on wearing would probably be little frayed around the elbows. His wife, Sally, by comparison looked the epitome of elegance, and so, on average, they were rather smart. They made themselves useful without getting enmeshed in the detail; accomplished hosts indeed.

The great marble-pillared, cream stuccoed hall looked magnificent. Various urchins, mainly offspring of the Blankshire, had been recruited to wear tight black uniforms, take coats, and act as general wine waiters and all round poppets. Out in the grounds of the Big House, Bert and Don, two long time car based followers, characterised by a rather unfortunate approach to dental hygiene that meant they had rather less than one full set of teeth between them, had been supplied with bright fluorescent jackets and were in charge of parking. Their reward: ensuring the empty bottles were truly empty by the end of the evening.

The books themselves, the real excuse for the shindig, were stacked in neat piles. My long time personal assistant, Rebecca, wearing something that I'm sure was exceptional value but looked a million dollars, brought a touch of glamour to the sales desk. So the stage was set. The stagehands were ready; all that was needed now were some actors.

They were not long arriving, and almost first among them, never one to miss an opportunity to gawp at what the neighbours were up to, was the belted earl. He was quickly into the fray, to his credit buying five books. As his father and grandfather both featured prominently, it was a bit of a family album. Shortly afterwards Alex appeared, looking pukka with the immaculate Charlotte, imperious in her height and bearing. Flicking through the book, Alex said to the belted earl, "Ah, Sid! Good to see you." He muttered quietly to me, "The things people say for the sake of common civility," before again addressing his peer. "Been flicking through this book here, Sid. Good job, don't you think? Some nice pics here of your old dad. Funny, though, don't seem to see any of you. Mmm, wonder why that is, eh what?"

The belted earl, while a keen supporter of the Blankshire, was famously not a keen rider. Alex, having got this delicate little opening salvo in very effectively, swanned quickly on, for once leaving the belted earl with the whirring cogs.

So things were shaping up nicely. Lucy appeared on the arm of the long-suffering Nick, and accepted, in her charming mother-hen fashion, quite proper congratulations. The place was filling up, and for once I could see why people thought country life glamorous. Col, who looked after my horses, was liberated from muddy jeans and dirty boots in a surprisingly stylish new suit. Debonair, dashing, brown eyes flashing, with his stable girl, Fiona, who was in skin tight jeans, a figure hugging check shirt, and pearls. Fiona in pearls? I had to look again. Without question she was underdressed for the occasion, but while her satorial skills were not the most polished, with a figure like Fiona's no man in the room would utter a word of complaint. A wistful sigh perhaps, until becoming aware of a stony look from the other half and realising further contemplation would mean the risk of an elbow in the tummy.

The soon to join the ancestors had turned out in force. For many of them it was an opportunity to see a house they had known for many years in the hands of William's dad coming back to life. I guess the past was joining them on an evening like this, watching a different generation enjoy what had been of such significance to them.

The till was ticking over at rare speed. We had printed 1,500 copies, and were selling them at what at the time seemed like an extortionate price of £5, but they were being snapped up: five copies here, seven there. It was all rather thrilling for the author of the whole event.

"Christmas presents for various great aunts? Job done," someone exclaimed with satisfaction.

"Perfect gift when we are invited out to dinner," said another clutching a further five copies, although knowing the limits of that particular social circle I suspected the recipients would already have their own copies.

The food now being served was timely. Those driving had been sipping genteelly; those who were not driving, however, were glugging frenetically away. The difference in behaviour between the two tribes, the gluggers and the sippers, was beginning to become apparent.

Dave, a local race horse trainer and stalwart, brave rider, had been known at the end of evenings such as this to remove his trousers and set them on fire for reasons even he couldn't remember. Perhaps excusable in a young man, but he was now approaching forty. Tonight he clearly had the car keys (and a good thing too, I thought to myself) as, for once, he was among the ranks of the sippers. His wife, Alison, had clearly been glugging, and was standing far too close to the belted earl, explaining in stentorian tones how poor the staff up at his stud were and how he should organise things. This rant was greeted in stony silence, which sadly only redoubled her efforts to explain her point.

I watched from the sidelines and enjoyed the evening unfolding. We had reached the semi formal bit of the evening, as no occasion such as this could be free of a speech or two, and it was my role to act as master of ceremonies. BOOOSSHH! The huge echo of the gong once used to call the house to dinner faded, and the spotlight turned on me… but only briefly.

I was about to speak, but the belted earl, as Chairman of the hunt committee, decided to steal the moment. He had something to say (he always did, most of his closest acquaintances would add), and stood in my limelight to say it.

"Sally and William, Lords and Ladies," the earl gave a self satisfied grin "Lucy and Hector, ladies and gentleman. It's wonderful to see such a crowd of you here tonight." As he launched into his "spontaneous" oration I was only half listening, more concerned with how many of my carefully prepared sentiments he was about to steal. He went on at some length, and then, "And, of course, the purpose of the evening is to help us get the stables back in good order. Obviously a huge amount of work has been done. Everyone's shifted themselves, and, working it out roughly on the back of an envelope, I reckon tonight we've made around £5,000. So that's a huge vote of thanks to good old Hector G and his hardworking team, especially Lucy – if I may say, the real brains behind the enterprise." Just when I thought we were home without controversy, he added, "But that still leaves us, or rather you lot, with another £30k to go. I reckon that's going to be pretty tough for all of you. Best of British." And on that supremely unhelpful note, he concluded.

The polite applause faded quickly. I moved to thank him and in turn accept his thanks. It was important to get this right, but only for the sake of good and proper form, and then to spread the thanks with rather greater liberality, as I did. I realised the point he had made in such an ill chosen way was, unfortunately, a good one, but for now it was time to don a happy face. Flowers for Lucy and Sarah, and thanks all round. A few silly jokes from me, and the bulk of the evening was done.

The gluggers were snatching freshly charged glasses whenever the attention of the sippers slipped, aware the happy time was drawing to an end. The attitude seemed if there were to be recriminations for glugging, they might as well be fully earned. In the meantime, part of me was chattering to those of an older generation as they told me of the fascinating world created by the belted earl's dad, who had spent the ancestors' cash with a liberality wholly alien to his son, while another part of my mind was asking itself the all important question. OK, five grand was in the bag, but where in the name of hell were we going to get the other thirty thousand from?

NINE

The Soliloquy

THE LIFE OF the evening was ebbing, and the gluggers were finally being separated from the object of their desire. Bert and Don were emptying the cars from the park, and would shortly be intent on doing the same with the contents of the various bottles. Those of more vintage years had taken one last nostalgic look around the old house and shuffled quietly away into the night.

I felt a bit of a crash coming. What needed to be done had been done: the county had come together and enjoyed a party, and now I too had to face the cold of the night. Common sense had suggested a local taxi be arranged for 10pm, although such had been my concentration that I had drunk practically nothing and would have happily driven home. The anointed hour had almost arrived, and I was prepared to wander out to see if the taxi was around when William appeared, a decanter in hand.

"I say, Hector, good show. All went as well as could be expected. Great to have the house heaving again. I think you and I deserve a proper drink now, what do you say? Don't worry about your taxi car thingy, I'll make sure Bert or Don" (who were lurking in the background, contentedly pouring the dregs of various bottles into one magnum) "don't let the bugger go without you. I think we've earned something a bit special."

We headed into the study and each took a seat in two large armchairs facing the fire, which was burning down now. Its energy, like the evening, was slipping away. The study was a quiet room, gently lit, with pools of darkness between the lights, and portraits of the past gathering round in the shadows to listen. Again I sensed I was about to become fate's instrument.

"What I have here is some fine whisky. Now then, the point of this little treat is to help you sort out a conundrum. From the Isle of Jura – the whisky not the conundrum, obviously. I recommend it as long as we don't go mad. Bad head day otherwise. Do try a glass." At this he poured us both an exceptionally large measure.

"You see, Hector, you've been around here for a few years now. People like you, they trust you. You get things done, and yet you're not one of us. No bad thing either, by the way. Too many of 'us' round here if you ask me, but that's another story." I had no clear idea where the conversation was going. "Your dealings with the Ladies' Racquets Club: masterful! Most people in your situation would have hurled toys everywhere. Took me years to realise total capitulation and then rebuilding from the ground up is the only way with that lot, but you got it in an afternoon. Tremendous!"

"Anyway, point of all this, it has to be said, is that we all get huge fun from riding with the Blankshire. Never quite know what's going to happen next. Who'd go to Switzerland skiing when they can pop out of their front door and have twice the thrill? And it's good that we have embarked on this quest to rebuild the stables. Fact is that Alex's family have done a lot for the Blankshire over the years, and we have collectively let the place go to rack and ruin. Big question is: how do we get the 'us' around here to fund the rebuilding job? Now I reckon that Alex will, of his own volition, supported by Charlotte – not such a bad old bird really once you resign yourself to agreeing with her I find. What do you think? Anyway, back to the point. I reckon Alex will come up with some bright idea, but it will be dependent upon the rest of us to help finance it.

"Tricky thing is none of us want to put our hands in our pockets generally, and certainly not if we don't think the others are going to. Now Sid, the belted earl to you, is without question extra well clued up on the price of everything, but is not really a man who is big on the value of things. He is also determined not to follow the path of his dad, who did know how to spend. Bright fellow, Sid. A lot going on in that head of his, you know. Too much so for the likes of me to get a grip on, anyway.

"So our conundrum, as I see it, is how do you talk some sense into people who just won't listen? It's my experience that all of us big landowners, while outwardly very different, are in one essential way the same. When it comes to the inheritance, the land and so on, we spent a number of years growing up being told who we are and how we are to live our lives." Here he waved vaguely at the pictures on the wall. "Their will must be obeyed, you know. No opposition is brooked. We hated it, of course, then one day we all discovered we were on our own and were free to do exactly as we chose. And do you know what? By then we had already decided that not listening was going to be our thing too. As a result, when it comes to our personal affairs I'm afraid to say we make a really bad audience. We like to tell, but we don't like to listen.

"Tonight was a classic example. Obvious you were all set up with a touching, friendly little speech, which would have been the only appropriate thing, and what happens? Bugger me, the Hon Chairman has to get up on his hind quarters, uninvited, and not only pinch all your best lines but ramble on at us for ten minutes. I personally thought it was a bit inappropriate. Sure he would have been told not to, but the desire to hear his own voice was just too overwhelming. Absolutely typical!

"Now, the stables. A couple of us have already marked out our positions, and those positions are not very helpful. You see, this not listening thing is a really big problem. We listen to each other, but that's only so we can go home and tell the missus what bloody fools the others are. Generally we listen to our bank managers. We pay 'em a lot of money, and this is a rather nice way to live. I keep busy ensuring the family fortune stays there or thereabouts, and I am rather good at it too."

At this point, William had a gulp of his whisky, until then almost untouched. "Finally, of course we listen to our wives. More than they think, although not as much as they'd like. So, you might well ask – more whisky by the way?" I nodded, a further huge slug was poured into my glass, then William continued.

"So, question is how do you influence us? I don't just mean me, I mean the belted earl, the Bicester family, and the other half dozen or so who could between 'em resolve this in an afternoon. I've given it all some thought, chatted to a few others about it. Struggling to remember what they had to say, but no mind. Anyway, one other thing we all care about is our standing. Everyone knows us, and we know everyone – everyone of any consequence, that is. Have to say a lot more people know me than vice versa, but I guess that's just an occupational hazard, eh? It might sound a bit feudal, but it's not that long since people like me could kick someone on to the streets at no notice. To some of us it was only the day before yesterday, but, and this is the important point, the regard of our peers is very important. The one thing none of us can stand is to be laughed at. Our self-regard is crucial to us. Sure you've noticed, you're a pretty shrewd fella. You do need to think in terms of a little people management. You've done pretty well so far getting us all on side, but if you're going to find that thirty grand, or whatever the figure is, you'll have to do a bit more."

There was a silence. The clock ticked and the fire sighed; ash fell as coal shifted, moving quietly towards the bottom of the grate.

"So, Hector, by a mixture of tools, largely ones people won't notice, you and I are going to have to find a way to promote a rapprochement between Alex and the belted earl. If we – you – can find a way of squaring them off, I reckon I can get the others to do their bit to find the money needed. How does that sound to you? Practical? Possible? As the outsider, you'd be surprised at your influence."

At that moment Sally appeared, silhouetted by the light from the hall. "William, are you in here with the whisky? Is that a good idea?" Sally was, for this evening at least, of the sipper persuasion.

William replied happily, seemingly none too bothered at the charge of secret whisky drinking, "Don't worry, darling, Hector and I have just been putting the world to rights. Or at least, I have. Hector has been very patient, and mainly listened."

"Oh Hector, I'm sorry. Don't tell me, William has been banging on at you, outlining his daft theories, not letting you get a word in edgeways. He has, hasn't he?"

Difficult one, this, so I decided it was a statement rather than a question. We both knew what William could be like, so we just exchanged knowing grins.

"I think my taxi's here, anyway. Thank you both very much, wonderful evening. I've got plenty to think about, that's for sure. William actually made a huge lot of sense, if only this once!" The whisky felt pretty good, too. I lurched, a distinct roll in my gait, towards the door with a new sense of confidence. This clear offer of help from William meant at least one of them was now properly on my side.

TEN

An Interlude

FOLLOWING MY LITTLE bravura performance at the book launch, the tentacles of my past reached out to grab me. I was due to meet up with my two main partners in crime at my former firm, the Universal Deadweight Shipping Company Limited, or the "DWs" as they styled themselves.

Ralph Threepunce and Andy Hobson, sophisticated men of business, the DW's had built up over 20 years a very successful shipping business. By a remarkable combination of flattery and intelligent analysis the DWs had, time after time, demonstrated the old maxim that a fool seldom gets to spend much time relaxing in the company of his money. I had worked with them on several projects over the years; we'd had our wins and our failures, and the occasional truly spectacular financial wipe out. While their reputation in the city was somewhat colourful the DW's had never been other than rigorously fair with me. We had won; we had argued; we had fallen out and made up. Blame didn't interest them. "What next?" was always their question. Did they still like you? Was there a rapport? They lived in the present and dreamed only of the future. If they talked of the past at all, it was to disinter their younger selves and to prod with awed amusement at quite how wild (and foolish) they had been. Their late night tales of the past were just that: to be produced late at night for amusement. For the daylight hours their concern was the present and the future, particularly the latter.

I remained on the list of people whose opinion they valued. I was not consulted too often or at great length, but we all enjoyed the relationship and its history of success. These days we met but twice a year, lunching well in the summer, and then the big occasion: a day's shooting every year in the hills above Norwich. This was close to where Andy Hobson had been born, and his brother, Chris, was still a gamekeeper on a local shooting estate. The actual spot we had chosen to shoot, or rather Andy had chosen, was the estate of a ship owning client, so we were returning a favour.

The format was always the same. A dinner the night before with various friends, old and new, and the star turn, the self proclaimed international athlete and shooting legend, Albert Holloway. His reputation had grown since our first meeting. With supernatural eye and calm manner that suggested ice in the veins, he had now represented Great Britain on numerous occasions, and, although only thirty-eight, was tipped for further Olympic success. While some might initially be inclined to doubt his claim to international sporting superstardom – there can be few Olympic champions who tip the scales at twenty-three stone – he was a phenomenon and a legend in his small world of clay pigeon shatterers.

It was these three who, consciously or otherwise, drove the dynamic of the day: Ralph was the oh so modest king; Andy the regent, disposing as Ralph proposed; and Albert, without question, the licensed jester. It was his role to ensure the conversation flowed and that guests were entertained, and were entertaining. Those of a nervous or pompous disposition seldom attended twice.

We were gathered in the front dining room of the Hotel Wimborne a little after eight, chatting quietly, those in the know anticipating the inevitably late entrance of Albert. Almost on cue, there was a crash as the front door was flung open, a clatter of bags being dropped, then the familiar stentorian tones of Albert launched into his hyperbolic introduction to the hotel receptionist:

"You don't know me, but I'm Albert Holloway, international sporting legend and highly trained Olympic athlete. You 'ave a room reserved for me, with a bigger bed for the bigger chap as usual...?"

"Ah yes, the beach ball has arrived," observed Andy waspishly. He was the only man on earth who was permitted to make such observations and live to tell the tale.

Albert swaggered into the room. The silly grin on his face told me he knew how ridiculous this approach was, and how much he was enjoying it. He could take himself seriously, but why bother on a night like this when there was fun to be had? Never designed by nature to be slim, he had the frame of a well-fed carthorse, and as always he was rumbustious.

"Chaps, chaps," he cried, "evening! You'll never guess what? They've named some champagne after me. look, look!" Brandishing a brace of bottles in his enormous ham of a hand, he invited us to inspect. Sure enough, they were labelled La Maison Holloway. "So what do you lot think of that, then? Anyone else in the room got a champagne cuvée named after 'em?"

Silence.

"Nope, thought not. I'd better share mine then." Within seconds corks had flown, and we were able to taste the latest homage to M'ssr Holloway, the candlestick maker's son from the back streets of Norwich.

"Not bad, eh? Good for serving to all those Greek shipowners you keep producing, Andy. Cor, what larks we shall have tomorrow."

Albert joined the throng. As usual he sat next to me, keeping up an unrelenting stream of comments across the table. His career, from its sponsorship in the early days by Andy, was taking off, but he was still keen to develop it further. As well as shooting for his country in the summer, he ran one of the best shoots in the country in the winter. What he had achieved in a short space of time was remarkable. His place in the Norfolk hills was not ideal, but by dint of guile, salesmanship, and sheer hard work he had built up a reputation and was on his way to becoming international. He had not yet entertained the crowned heads of Europe, but it was only a question of time.

Ever since our first meeting, some four years earlier, Albert and I had got on. We would exchange confidences and ask each other's advice. In amongst the fast flowing banter at the table, Albert chatted to me conspiratorially.

"See, the thing is, 'Ector, this place tomorra, I know the chap that owns it. Nice enough fella, but 'e 'as this almost new 'ead keeper chap. Not impressive. He's only twenty-five, and he's a posh public school gadger. Yer know, all that crap, posh voice, but as far as I can see not a 'hwful lot up top. Thinks he belongs with the guns, forgets 'is place. Terrible mistake if you ask me." Albert did not have a lot of truck with the quality trying to fill his particular niche in life,

"Now you see, I have a dilemma. Being the bloke I am people watch me, so if the birds don't fly right, by which I mean high and difficult, I will be obliged to hignore 'em. Albert does NOT shoot low birds. Everyone 'oo is anyone knows that. Mein host, not being a proper shooting man himself, might see it as being a bit bloody rude of me, but everyone else will notice that I'm ignoring the low birds and deduce, quite correctly, that the new fella ain't doin' it right.

"If, on the other hand, I do decide to get stuck in, which I assuredly won't, then I will be doing the decent thing but, and it's a big but, the beaters will think I've gone soft. Bloody bush telegraph, they are. They'll tell all and sundry that Albert's not what he was, picking off the low birds just to keep 'is score up – as if I would! So my reputation, been years abuilding it up, will be done no good at all, just 'cos some chinless wonder is too full of 'is own importance to learn and take a few tips."

This dilemma explained, he then launched into a particularly improbable story for the whole table of what befell a peer of the realm unwise enough to wager Albert that he could navigate the walls of a snooker room without touching the floor. An ambulance for the peer and victory for Albert was, inevitably, the outcome. As always, one story led to another, and various confessions of comic idiocy followed. Even Ralph, normally the most taciturn of men on group occasions, was persuaded to launch forth about the unsavoury lavatorial habits of the original owner of the Universal Deadweight Shipping Company.

By one in the morning the company was in varying degrees of merriment. In an Irish court we would have been pronounced "Of the drink they had a taken", and so we slipped off quietly to bed.

ELEVEN

Everyone Hop

I T WAS A good shooting day. This meant that the rain had just about stopped and there was a fair wind blowing. The birds would be more inclined to fly high, making them a proper challenge.

We gathered for breakfast, and the shoot owner, Phil Cass, joined us, together with Albert's bête noir.

"My name is Head Keeper Timothy Smythe-Ward, but Tim to all of you. You'll be having a topping day with my birds." So his introduction went. He was enthusiasm itself, greeting all of us, with the notable exception of Albert, like long lost friends, standing a little too close, chuckling over his own wan jokes, and pronouncing again and again we were set for a "terrific day". I could even feel my mild mannered hackles rising.

Albert, on the other hand, was largely ignored by Timothy. That the dynamic between them was not of the most positive sort was patently obvious. They circled each other; if they had been dogs some suspicious and unsavoury sniffing would have taken place.

I climbed into the same car as Ralph and Albert. It was a twenty minute drive up to the estate itself, and, full of rather good English breakfast, we lapsed into a companionable silence. Finally Ralph, curious as always, could resist no longer, and peppered Albert with a barrage of questions.

"Well, Albert, what do you think is going on? You really don't appreciate young Timmy, do you? I mean, I'm not over particular, but he did seem a bit on the matey side. Not quite proper I thought, but I dunno about this stuff."

"Yeah well, Ralph, you're new to this shooting lark. Let me tell you, in fifteen years of running my own shoot I have yet to EVER, and I mean EVER, find the time to join the guns for breakfast. I mean, the last thing they want to see is me a-loomin' out of the early morning mist at 'em, and, far more important, I'm out and about, aren't I? Checking the weather, that all the beaters are present and correct, we 'ave enough ammo, getting an idea which birds are to be found where, and so on. To be honest, it's never ending. I mean, I reckon you silly lot have paid a pretty big wedge for a day in my company and on my gaff, and it's my job to make sure you go 'ome with your tail up and a smile on your face. Least ways, if you don't it's cos you've shot like a twat, and therefore it's not my fault."

"You're saying you're not really a great fan of young Timmy, aren't you, Albert?" Ralph sometimes asked the most obvious of questions; often, I suspected, to perpetuate the conversation.

"Well, if you want my honest opinion, and just between us, if I was organising an arse kicking competition I'd sooner put my money on the one legged man to win it than 'im. However, I judge a man by what he produces. Let's just say, at the moment I would not be expecting anything too great. Don't go getting your hopes up."

Ralph thought a last word was necessary. From a man whose credo in life was never to fall out with anyone for less than twenty million sterling, I expected exactly what I heard. "Look, Albert, I know you're not impressed and I understand your impatience, but let's just smile and enjoy, shall we?"

For once, Albert suffered being spoken to. "Yes, boss," he said, and lapsed into a silence that was not gruntled.

To those who know them, the hills just outside Norwich provide some spectacular shooting. We were dropped off at the bottom of a dry valley, wooded and rising away from us, which should have been a good spot. In theory, the birds would be driven over us. Our host, Mr Cass, stood behind us so he could enjoy the sight of justice being done to his lovingly nurtured birds.

I imagined how the day should go as I unsleeved my gun, waiting for the first drive itself to begin. We were positioned, eight of us in a line about fifty yards from each other, in the valley bottom facing towards the higher side. As we settled ourselves, a military style operation should be taking place beyond the valley top. Fifteen to twenty people, the beaters, would be moving through the undergrowth with sticks and staves, whistling, calling, crashing and bashing.

If the head keeper had done his job properly, this hulla-baloo should encourage the birds, pheasants and partridges in the main, to fly away from the noisy intruders and over us. Standing beyond us was a small battalion of green clad country dwellers, equipped with a variety of dogs. They were known, rather unimaginatively, as the picker-uppers, as it was their job to pick up the shot birds. It was also their self-assumed role to judge the ability of the guns, and they were the starting point of Albert's feared bush telegraph. They missed little, and talked a lot.

So, if the machinery of the shoot was in place, the rest was up to the individual guns. However, and it is always a big however, everything depended upon the competence of the head keeper, in this case the beloved Timmy. If the con-ditions had not been assessed accurately the beaters would be in the wrong place, and the birds, if present, would not fly over the guns. Wasted drives meant unhappy customers, and, in our case, a vindicated international sporting legend.

A whistle blew. I knew the theory, now to see how Timmy delivered in practice. All was quiet, then a bird or two appeared, one flying high and heading towards Andy, stationed thirty yards down from me. Gun up; on bird; past bird; bang! One for the bag, then silence again. Motionless figures, hunched over their guns, waited, and waited, and waited. Seconds turned into minutes, then multiples of minutes...still nothing.

Things were, to put it mildly, not going to plan. Indeed, at that moment all we had was plenty of nothing. Then I heard it: the mass fluttering of disturbed and angry pheasants. A great flock appeared, wheeling, rising, and turning above the tree line; to the cognoscenti, a bouquet of pheasants. Hundreds of the damn things, and they were heading away from any of our guns. Other birds flew low over the line, not fifty yards above, which is as it should be, but more like ten or twenty yards. Cruelly easy, even for guns of our very mixed abilities.

One or two of us were unable to resist, so the firing began and birds did fall from the sky. Challenging, however, it was not. This drive was frustrating. My pulse remained untroubled by the need to race; there was the odd bird worth the point and fire treatment, but truthfully it was painful. It was like opening a bottle of champagne and discovering most of the bubbles had been omitted.

I glanced over to see what Albert was making of all this. Unlike the rest of us, who were standing, Albert was plonked thirty yards down from me on a special contraption: his very own customised shooting stick. With what appeared to be a small tractor tyre attached to the top end, this stick allowed him to rest his not inconsiderable behind while waiting for the action to begin.

"Invented it myself, of course. Not a lot of call for

something of this size," he said, pointing at the tyre end of his shooting stick. "Not everyone has my 'ealthy appetite, you see." He sat solemn, impassive, a great green clad Buddha; occasionally deigning to raise his gun, but generally leaving well alone. Knowing as I did that high birds were his game, I was not surprised. Short of breaking his gun over his knee, it was difficult to know how he could have made a more emphatic point.

The rest of the guns continued to amuse themselves as best they could, one or two of them only recognising a low bird as one sauntering on the ground, so the bag was mounting, but not in the way a real sportsman could enthuse about. After the drive had finished there was the usual joie de vivre, but it felt rather like rejoicing at an Arsenal one-all draw. Fans might like it, but for the cognoscenti it wasn't really what it was all about.

At the conclusion of this, the first of five drives scheduled for the day, little Timmy appeared, rubbing his hands together in his slightly oily and over familiar public school fashion. "Well, chaps, did we all enjoy that? Bit tough for you, were they, Albert?" The chin removal surgery had worked well for Timmy. A bit of a wonder, in fact – I could feel Albert's shudder of contempt from thirty yards away.

As we got to the next drive I was partnered next to a plump and prosperous partner in a firm of city solicitors. Unusually, the two of us were to begin the drive standing very close to one another.

Timmy wandered up to us. "See, you two look very happy there. You'll be ever so pleased if they ever introduce gay marriages properly, I'm sure!" It was not the gay innuendo we disliked so much as its source and its sheer limpness.

This second drive ran no more successfully than the first one. Albert was still staging his version of a sit down strike, and the high birds, such as they were, again flew out of range. As the drive continued, things went from bad to worse. There was a great flush of birds, but sadly 200 yards south of us, leaving the guns collectively staring at the empty sky in front of them. A solitary duck appeared way out of range overhead, quacking mournfully and providing what was beginning to sound like a requiem for the day.

A hooter sounded to bring the drive, and the torment, to an end. As predicted, our host, Mr Cass, in his naivety had little idea of the real problems. All he knew was Albert wasn't responding to the display of birds.

"Do you think Albert's all right? Not doing well on the bag, not well at all. With his reputation and everything, I'd have thought he'd tuck in. Been some nice easy ones too, even I could have done better!" It was like hearing a learner driver suggesting he could teach Stirling Moss a thing or two about accelerating out of a hairpin bend.

In the meantime, Albert had adopted silence as the best policy, but it was clear this was at considerable cost to his outgoing personality. A great thundercloud of tension was clearly building, and our host couldn't see it for looking, never mind work out how to discharge it. This could only end in tears, and I was willing to bet they wouldn't be Albert's. The picker-uppers behind me knew something was not right. They were chatting earnestly to each other, heads nodding, a little bit of pointing. Albert, as always, was the centre of attention, but for once he might have wished to swap his shooting stick for a cloak of invisibility.

After this drive ended we went back to the Land Rovers. Picnic baskets appeared with coffee, delicious nibbles, and, for those who wanted it, sloe gin. I suddenly became aware that Albert's looming presence was absent. Curiously, only I had noticed the disappearance of the human beach ball. Something was up, I'd guess; either that or he'd finally popped, and if that was the case I'm sure we'd have heard the bang.

Some twenty minutes later, most of us were replete and wandering towards the next drive when Albert quietly reappeared. Inscrutable, he winked at me as we tramped to our places. There was the usual wait, laced with apprehension at the thought of another fiasco. Time for me to take in the scenery and contemplate my good fortune. There were many worse ways to spend a Tuesday.

This drive was a bit slow to start. I raised my gun, lowered it, and made a few practice mounts. I noticed little Timmy, behind the guns as usual, glancing at his watch and tapping it. Did I detect a hint of nerves? A touch of impatience? With a rather undignified scowl he raised his walkie talkie, then as he did so, instead of the usual ragged sound of the distant, hollering beaters came a roar of noise, a tsunami of sound washing down the valley, Timmy looked up, baffled.

Now in quickening pace the birds began to appear, and this time they were flying over our heads, high and true. The guns began to shoot, and at last Albert felt able to join in. Difficult? Yes they were, but memorable, and of course that's the point. The moment of suspense as the trigger pulls, and with a good shot, a connection. A small puff of feathers spelling instant extinction for the luckless bird, wheeling out of the sky, then a dog appears to retrieve what is now a Sunday roast to be.

The drive continued, and all thoughts of other people's birds and the inadequacies of the wretched Timmy were gone. The only thoughts were about how to reload quickly. Fumbling fingers, cartridges showering onto the ground, breech of gun closed again, sharp click. Another covey of birds, partridges this time, high again, small and jinking, distant but doable. Bang, crump, flutter, bounce. The ragged sound of firing echoed up and down the valley. All the guns were obtaining good sport: wonderful priceless champagne sport, as it should be. It's what they live for. Albert, now a cordon bleu chef presented for the first time with some quality ingredients, was on his feet, moving with astonishing speed and grace for such a large man. Economical and effective in his movements, accounting for much more than his fair share, his reputation was now being burnished and not tarnished.

The horn went to mark the end of the drive, and the guns gathered, now genuinely full of excited chatter.

"Did you see that one?"

"Both barrels!"

"Not seen birds like those for eons."

"Swear that last one was so high it had snow on its back."

And, remarkably, this state of affairs continued over the next two drives. The huge whoop to signal the beaters were moving, the wonderful show of high birds where they should be, and Albert showing his talents to their best. The owner of the estate was beside himself with glee, while young Timmy had the complacent pride of ownership written all over his face.

Only Albert was quiet. Stoic. Shooting like this was what he did. A workman now, taking pride in a job well done: high birds cleanly dispatched. No elation for him; it wouldn't be proper in front of the amateurs.

Still, I knew something was not right. We'd had a great day, but I strongly suspected we had little to thank Timmy for.

Finally, after the shoot tea of shepherd's pie, red wine, and ribald remarks, the guns began to sort themselves for departure. "Want a lift, young 'Ector?" volunteered Albert. "I can take you as far as Stowmarket, and you can catch the train from there."

We climbed into the car and set off into the night.

"Now then, Albert, I know you fixed something. What I need to know is what?"

"Well, you remember my dilemma?"

"Of course I do."

"Thing is, neither Timmy nor his boss actually bother to superintend what's going on. The boss don't know how, and Timmy's far too busy trying to hobnob with you lot to actually run around and do a proper job of work. Now, just think. You've seen me on a day down at Tingley." Tingley was Albert's own shoot. "'Ow much of me do you see during a day?"

I remembered my days at Tingley. The only thing ever to be seen of Albert was the sight of him clad totally in a vast green plastic shroud, splattered with mud, zipping about the place on a beat-up quad bike. Anywhere and everywhere, shouting down the walkie talkie at errant beaters or stray picker-uppers. The only place he is never seen is with the guns, other than perhaps roaring up briefly to trade abuse with Andy

"Not a lot."

Ignoring me, he continued, in full flow now, "Well, I'll tell you 'ow much of me you see. Nothing is 'ow much. This young pup Timmy, on the other hand, is too busy mucking in and 'avin' 'is three 'apence worth with you lot. Clear to me 'e wouldn't notice a little constructive help from me. Only problem was how to persuade the head beater to take one or two suggestions on board. He's a local lad, not keen to disobey the boss. Good chap, loyal too, and quite right I may add. He and I were chatting, as you do, and I told him about the Albert Hop."

All right, I knew with Albert the tale would not be a simple one. This was lining up to be ever so slightly preposterous.

"Go on, tell me what the Albert Hop is." I recoiled inside; no doubt it would be devious and utterly effective.

"Well, what I explained to him is, 'Look, chap, been thinking. Yer know, on top of anything old Timmy boy might 'ave mentioned to yer, there's a decent breeze blowing today. Yer might like to try the Albert Hop'. Dead curious 'e was straight away. Of course, I knew 'e would be, so I explained. 'For the Albert Hop to work my instructions have to be followed to the letter. Best get 'em to rehearse it,' I told 'im.

"Follow the youngster's orders, then march 250 yards to the right. When the instruction to begin the drive comes stay steady, count to 200, slowly mind, then do the Albert Hop. This involves bouncing up and down, high as you can go, and giving a great big shriek. Just like you do to start a normal drive, but much, much louder. Then crack on as usual, but with real added vigour.' I told him it was my trade secret. Never let me down yet, it ain't. Was only sharing it with him because things were not quite going as they might be. Anyway, fella was pretty desperate by then. First job and all. No doubt 'oo Timmy would be blaming. He's gotta blame someone, and the head beater would be right at the front of the queue. Those first two drives, shocking...words fail me..."

The expressions playing over Albert's face as he spoke were a symphony of contempt.

"Of course, fella was fascinated. I do 'ave a certain reputation, you know! Told him he had to brief all the beaters about the whole plan, and count on Timmy being out of the way with the guns."

"Well, Albert," I said, marvelling at his ingenuity, "it seemed to work, I have to say. Just one thought: if no one else uses the Albert Hop or anything like it, how did you come to discover it?"

"Discover it? I just made it up on the spot. That's why it's never let me down! Thing was, the beaters were so worried about doing the Albert Hop right, they completely ignored the fact that they had moved 250 yards to the right, contrary to boss's instructions, makin' decent allowance for the breeze blowin' that Timmy seemed to be ignorin'. This was what I really wanted. The extra noise was just icin' on the cake, and it bloody well worked, didn't it, young 'Ector?"

He gave me a great big grin, and in that moment a plan for the future crystallised in my head.

TWELVE

The Wagon

I WAS BACK in Blankshire country, still savouring the excitement of the shooting day and the sheer devilment of the Albert Hop. However, the bigger plan, my plan, would take time and a particular conjunction of the stars to deliver. I would need to discuss it with the unwitting source of its inspiration, Albert, whose role would be key. Also I would need to use my powers of persuasion, so glowingly described by William, to enlist the help of one or two of "them" in the Blankshire county. All this would take time and some very careful thought.

However, the Lord of Misrule, also known as Murphy's Law, was not about to sit idly by and let things develop smoothly.

The initial spanner aimed fairly and squarely into the works originated, ironically enough, in a tired old Ford lorry, registration number LMR 38A, owned at that stage by Lettice. Curiously, despite her exuberant manner, forceful personality, and huge organisational skills, she was, at home, a pussycat. Possibly over aggression abroad was a compensation for meekness at the hearth; a bit like the Germans, some would say. Her husband, Malcolm, was a hugely, almost unreasonably, urbane man of an ancient Blankshire family. Eton education, a good degree, and a stratospheric career with a particularly smart and blue-blooded firm of Stockbrokers showed there was life yet in his particular gene pool. He sparkled and amused in equal proportions, a diamond of a man. He would put his arm around your shoulder, wander you over to the bar, whether you wanted to be there or not, and buy you a drink. If your choice was a diet cola, it was his pleasure to buy it. It always felt as though it was you he was interested in, not just another drink for himself. No wonder he was so adept at building the trust of his clients. And yet Lettice, the powerful domineering Lettice, became in his company a mouse. It was "Yes, Malcolm" this, "No, Malcolm" that, which seemed most curious to this outside and unmarried observer.

Lettice's long-standing craving, not satiated to date, was to convert her horse-shifting vehicle, a farm lorry in essence, into a proper Wagon with a capital W. Not generally given to boasting or displays of wealth, Lettice desired this symbol of modernity, complete with a "'Lectric up and down ramp" rather than her lift and heave job, and a little cooker where tea and hot mince pies could be served up. A piece of mobile domestic tranquility was her heart's desire. And yet Malcolm, "the brute" according to Lettice, was resolute. No and all its alternatives were repeated, frequently and often.

"After everything I've done for that man, too," Lettice whimpered to me one day, most unlike her.

At this point the annual MOT inspection of LMR 38A intervened, and the diagnosis was quick and to the point. "This vehicle is kaput. The cost of repairing it exceeds its economic value. We cannot recommend any more money is wasted."

Now, at last, Lettice had a case. A quick conversation ensued because we were, after all, in mid season, and time without a horse shifter was time wasted. So a deal between Malcolm and Lettice was done: if she could shift the horse shifter, the purchase of a proper wagon would be sanctioned.

At this point, Col inadvertently walked into what turned out to be a rather awkward trap. Col's horse shifter had, by reputation, assisted Noah in delivering animals to the ark. Even as a working artifact one felt it needed dignity not use. Col, who was usually prepared to suffer almost any amount of inconvenience rather than part with hard earned cash, had finally grasped the idea that something had to be done, and that the something would necessarily involve expenditure.

As I finished hunting for the day, I slid off my horse to land in the middle of a scene entitled "Something Being Done". Col and Lettice were enthusiastically shaking hands for a reason soon to emerge. Colin wandered over, and he was animated.

"You'll never guess what? Lettice has agreed to sell me her old truck. The body is in good nick, so I reckon all I need to do is get a decent chassis, which is easy, and I'll be the proud owner of something that is more than rust and mud. I mean, just look at poor old Mabel there." Why the Colin family had insisted on giving a name to their rust pile was beyond me, but Mabel she was and Mabel she remained in her dotage. "Poor old girl. And the price, well, it's really very reasonable indeed. Almost beyond reasonable." The relief was palpable. A glance behind at Mabel showed how urgently Colin Enterprises Inc needed something slightly less ancient. "And the thing is, Hector, I reckon" here he glanced at me sheepishly "her fellows might have been a bit pessimistic in their diagnosis. You know, a few hours' work back at the farm, couple of new parts, and hey! We might just get it through its MOT. What do you think of that?"

"I think, Col, yes, but if you get it going again you'll

have a deeply unamused Lettice on your hands. Are you prepared for Lettice going rogue? We both know it's not a pretty sight. She can be ruthless. Thing is, Col, are you willing to risk those little button eyes boring into you? Unspoken but hurtful accusations? Know what I mean? Lettice on the war path is pretty scary."

"No, no, it'll be fine. She's always so charming whenever I talk to her."

"Col, look, not really my business, bit of care though. That charm is closely linked to Lettice getting her own way, and the tap of charm can be turned off pretty quickly, as I know to my cost. So if you get your new acquisition running in the way you hope, I'd be keeping a pretty low profile if I were you."

"S'pose...nah, I'll be fine. I'll keep it out of the way, and job's a good 'un! I'll just go on using Mabel here to bring you on the sort of days when Lettice appears, and anyway, even if she does see, I'm sure she won't mind." Col was clearly conflicted, but desire for this deal was paramount. Quite right too, I thought, but he was a little slow to realise that not everyone had his balanced views and essential decency.

I spotted Lettice. "Hector, guess what? Col has agreed to buy the old wagon! Think he's going to scrap the chassis straight away and mate the body to a new chassis. Paid me OK money for it. Malcolm will be so pleased when I tell him I got better than scrap value. I'm a good girl, tra-laa!" She span on the spot and practically waltzed in front of me.

"So it's now Col's wagon, isn't it?"

"Well, yes, and he'll scrap it or whatever, and I get my new wagon, all mod cons, and everyone's happy. It's nice for good things to happen to Col, don't you think, Hector? I've bestowed a favour!"

Both parties were far too happy to do any reflecting, and they were consenting adults after all. I had no desire to be the Eyeore at the party. Better, I decided, to imagine Colin chugging home, bathed in the warmth of a deal done well. No longer in the remedial class in terms of horse shifters, and with potential for improvement.

At this point a little business took me off the scene, and the next stage in the saga passed me by. Apparently, the new vehicle was quickly adopted into the heart of the Colin family, and, inevitably, given a name: Freda. Once it had a name, talk of scrapping dried up. Parts were acquired, long hours were sacrificed, and the new owners of LMR 38A concluded that the bar for passing the MOT had dropped from an impossible six foot to a very modest two foot six. As a result, Colin's plan to turn the horse shifter, discarded so casually by Lettice, into a runner took shape.

The plan had already come to fruition as we turned up at Gabo Cliffs early one bright October morning. It was cold, bone chillingly cold, with an east wind blowing, locally referred to as a lazy wind: too idle to go round one, it went straight through, chilling to the marrow. There were few people out. I parked my car and wandered to the meet. Unusually the gathering was not held on horses but on foot; much needed whisky was on offer, along with fresh nibbles. The farrier, an impossibly good-looking man called Richmond Morley, wandered up to me.

"Now then, Griffiths, fookin wind." This was one of his friendlier greetings. "Cut yer in 'alf, it could. 'Ope you've got yer undies on?" Well, there was no answer to that so I moved on. Lettice was there, along with the rest of the Monday regulars, chatting to the nearly toothless twosome, Bert and Don. Of Col, however, there was no sign.

Idle chatter: outlook for the day; dreadful weather; state of the new season in the farming world. All run of the mill conversation. It was actually a lovely day; once out of the wind it was almost pleasant. I chatted to Lettice, wondering if today was the right moment to try and draw her into the bigger plan.

"Morning, Lettice. Hear Col's pleased with his new acquisition."

"Is he? That's interesting. Damn thing still going, is it?"

"Well, yes. I gather he's still drawing the horses out of the engine, and they are powering it rather nicely."

"Hector, surely not! Tell me you're joking?"

"Lettice, have you ever accused me of unnecessary jokes?"

"Well, Hector, now you mention it, not sure you're a great one for any jokes."

"Thanks for that, Lettice."

"No, I meant...oh, anyway, you say it's still running?" Lettice paused, a thought had clearly struck her. "Hmm, that might mean...it's just, I've told Malcolm that..."

This was clearly sensitive stuff. Time to mosey on and bugger off while the going remained good. Clearly Lettice was not in a favour dispensing mood.

"I'll just go and find my horse, Lettice." Having made good my escape, the clock was now drawing on to towards 11am. My quadruped was needed urgently, but still no sign of Col. Those with horses were clambering on board, and I felt a little isolated. I wandered along the side of some farm sheds, and a little further, past the last wagons of the intrepid few, ears cocked, listening for the sounds of the knackered Mabel trundling down the road. Nope, nothing. Nada. Diddly squat. Hell! Where was he? I felt a twinge of concern now; he was always here. Then, Col himself suddenly appeared from around the next corner, signalling me over. Behind him was not Mabel, but the newly rejuvenated Freda.

"Quick, sir!" Not like Col to address me formally, so clearly something was up. "Mabel's broken down, had to use the new wagon." Of course, new was something of a relative term here. "It's a bit awkward. Had planned to use a twin wagon strategy for this season, you know, till the heat has died down a bit.

"Bit of luck, though. As I thought, I got it going again. Cost me, of course. Spent 250 quid, but my brother, James, did a lot of work, welding and who knows what else. Anyway, sailed through its MOT. Only trouble is, I'm not very keen on Lettice seeing us just yet, yer know? Remembering our little conversation. Let 'er get used to the idea by word of mouth, then I thought I should be OK." He didn't know Lettice as I did. "So, for now I thought I'd tuck myself out of the way." Well, that part of the plan I could go with.

The subterfuge worked, this time at least. Col helped Michael clamber down the ramp, and I slid on board, trotting to catch up and wincing as the cold wind bit. Richmond Morely was quite right: I felt my cheeks go numb.

However, the countryside was glorious: hilly and high. Difficult to believe within a mile or so there were cliffs falling away sharply to the sea. We passed along a lane, watching the hounds bury their noses in the gorse on the steep hillside. Lettice was on fine form. She was a busy one, Lettice. Committee here, charity ball there; prison visiting; day at the races; lord mayor. I had to say I felt tired just listening, but the great thing was she was so delightfully unpompous, turning to me with a big grin on her face. "And do you know, Hector? It can all be such a rush. Before now I've jumped on that train to London, settled down in my seat, checked – yes, I've got the fur coat, but did I remember the red satin knickers?"

Subsequent enquires among several male friends have failed to elicit a better riposte than my mumbled "I see". Then she was off again. I was still puzzling over her underwear observation and only half listening when she asked, "And how's Colin getting on with my old wagon. Well?

"Well, yes, yer know…" An awkward pause. Typical, I thought, the messenger on trial yet again. Verdict: death by firing squad if I'm not careful. However, in for a penny… "Still working. Not quite sure what his plans are regarding the MOT. Gather that must be coming up pretty soon."

"Not pretty soon. Actually it was last Tuesday." Lettice was tarter than unsweetened apple pie. "I do hope he's not going to embarrass me. My people swore blind it was done for, and it was only because of this that I persuaded Malcolm to buy me my lovely, shiny, new proper wagon. The thing is, Hector, Malcolm is a dear man, but his folks have hunted with the Blankshire and farmed around Goldthorpe since time immemorial – 1189 if I remember my legal history." Not a useful thought, but I could see where this was going. "And he has this terrible fear, not so much of spending money but of being seen to waste money and being taken advantage of. He's had to work so terribly hard to recover the fortune of the estate. His father, Aldous: terrible spendthrift. All fast women and slow horses.

"So, if Colin pops up with that wagon, and yes, I know it's only a tired old farm truck, but Malcolm will feel we have been taken advantage of. Or, even worse, that *I've* been taken advantage of, and then Malcolm will be sulky, grumpy, and generally impossible. It doesn't happen often, but when it does he is so difficult. There is no talking to him, he just doesn't listen, and, of course, once it wears off he pretends it never happened. I'm afraid it rather affects me too. As you know, I'm not the greatest sufferer of fools, and if Malcolm is in one of his 'bates', I'm afraid the well of human kindness rather dries up." She smiled, a mixture of sadness and apology. I wondered if this was the whole story, but for now let it go.

So the lines of potential conflict were being drawn. If and

when the news reached Malcolm that LMR 38A, also known as Freda, was perfectly roadworthy, the fallout would be uncomfortable at best. At the moment Lettice, and indirectly Malcolm, were key components in my plan. Her knowledge of the other traditional Blankshire players was essential in getting them to help, and her milk of human kindness was clearly at a premium. I pulled a rather unattractive face and considered my next steps. The harnessing of Lettice would have to wait for the right opportunity.

THIRTEEN

Carols

BEFORE THE LETTICE harnessing opportunity presented itself, however, came the Blankshire Carol Service: a tradition of considerable standing, and a very special event. It was held on the second Sunday in December in a small medieval church close to the hunt kennels. The church, framed by leafless trees, was situated on a small rise, set against the very last of the setting sun, the waxing crescent of the moon already visible in the cold azure sky.

The service always started at 3.30pm prompt – very prompt. As I walked towards the church at 3.28pm, I heard the plangent echoes of *Once In Royal David's city* strike up, sung as a solo by a child accompanied only by a wheezy church organ. I paused to listen, the evocation of Christmases past bittersweet in the gloaming. It was a peaceful, poetic moment. Locked for reasons of my choosing into this almost closed order of countryside dwellers, these moments of beauty were of incontestable value to me, so very different to the commercial life that had been my lot for many years.

I quietly slipped into the back of the church, the light now almost gone. My desire to avoid being spotted as the latecomer was helped tremendously by the efforts of the church's current incumbent, the Reverend Gervaise Sidderly:

a man of Holy Orders and the highest of high camp tastes. He had decreed this service was to be held as au naturelle as possible. Now aged, Gervaise had grown up in a world that was very different from the one he inhabited now. The church had traditionally offered a safe and often warm welcome to men whose sexual proclivities were a struggle for both themselves and society as a whole.

The church was gorgeous in the richness of its decorations, and also in the way the lighting was used. Not only was the altar candle lit, but so too was the body of the church. Great primitive eighteenth century wooden chandeliers, holding hundreds and hundreds of candles, had each been lowered by hand and then hoisted to a little above head height before the ceremony began. I gather it was something of a performance; it took around an hour to light all the candles from tapers, and spoke volumes of the role faith had played before the coming of electricity.

Gervaise had obviously spent many a happy hour working out the optimum position for the chandeliers: high enough to be over the heads of the tallest parishioners, but low enough to maximise the light they gave off. It was amazing the health and safety brigade tolerated such an approach, but this was the approach Gervaise insisted upon for continuing in his ministry. Such was the relationship with the parishioners and with the Bicester family that his wish for "The sweet, soft light of the candle bright, just as in the manger" was respected and welcomed. The result was marvellous in its flickering unworldliness; the banners and tapestries, accumulated over the years, were lit by the last of the daylight and the flicker of faint candlelight. A fairy realm was created where the shadowy architectural details of the church, in daylight rather pedestrian, now spoke of caves, castles, lost places, and fantastic wonders. A hint of incense reflected a far more exotic view of religion than anything one might have expected in remote and rural Blankshire. It was of little surprise that the large number of children present were unnaturally quiet; rapt; lost in imaginings.

I sat and marvelled at the intermeshing of the two cultures. Gervaise was, as always, in crisp white robes and a highly decorated surplice, and, as the organist launched into 'Silent Night,' we all stood. I enjoyed the melancholy nature of this carol, and glancing at the service sheet I realised we'd all get to fill our lungs and belt out bigger tunes later. As 'Silent Night' came to an end, the belted earl stood to read out the creation story. I half expected a guest appearance from the great man himself to feature in the story, perhaps a small cameo to make sure the good Lord got the details of the belted earl's bit of Blankshire just so, but in fairness he delivered it exactly as the writers of the King James bible had intended.

The service chugged on. Of course, this being Blankshire not everything could go perfectly. The organ struck up the opening chords of 'The Holly and the Ivy,' which was a pity because the choir was set for 'Oh Little Town of Bethlehem.' After a few chords and a valiant but vain attempt to sing one song to the tune of another, the organ wheezed to a halt and regained the sequence set out in the order of service.

Familiar hymns, readings from the King James bible, pious words for the poor in Africa, Lucy reading the very traditional gospel according to Luke featuring the manger, and then we got to the prayers. Gervaise was famous, and rightly so, for the scope and liberality of his compassion, as well as his enthusiasm for hunting. It was an unusual combination, but one that added weight and sincerity to his words. It also gave him the latitude to talk to an audience who appreciated his views, because they knew he was so very sound on the subjects that were most important to them.

As the service came to an end with a rousing burst of 'God Rest ye Merry Gentlemen', the electric light under the bell tower flickered on to reveal a table laden with warm mince pies, port and whisky. There was a good crowd, and we clustered around. The quantity of alcohol said everything about Gervaise's high church views.

Gervaise wandered up to me. "Evening, Master. So what did you think of our humble little celebration of the nativity? Bit different, what?"

"Gervaise, you know it's one of the highlights of my year. Those old wooden chandeliers, positive master stroke, although, must say, kind of you to leave torches on the pews for those whose eyes can no longer adapt to candlelight."

"We have to make the odd concession to modernity, dear boy, but it's the atmosphere that candlelight conjures up. One of the highlights of my year, too. A humble church for what was really a very humble event..." He lapsed into silence; he had said all that was needed about the meaning he had invested in this simple ceremony.

Lettice was nearby, and she smiled at me weakly. She was with Malcolm, the latter looking as suave and assured as ever. Lettice was clearly no nearer to explaining her embarrassment to him, and I assumed her smile was designed to encourage continuing silence on my part. The situation was becoming a bit absurd.

My arm was grabbed by Lucy, jolly and good hearted as ever. "Hector, good evening! So thrilling, the sale of the books. Do you know? I just cannot believe it, they've nearly sold out! We're so excited, isn't it wonderful? We think we will have made nearly £6,000. Quite marvellous, much better than I thought we'd do."

"Lucy, without your inspiration it would never have happened."

She blushed, most appropriately, and started talking

about all her helpers. Quite true too, but it was nice to see her happy and revelling in her status as a Blankshire queen bee. She, for one, had earned it.

At that point I felt a powerful hand on my arm, and turned to see Charlotte, all five foot ten of her. Wearing elegant court shoes, dark hair in a widow's peak, she was as well groomed as ever.

"Hector, Alex and I have been talking. I wonder, would you be kind enough to pop up to the house after this lot has finished? We have to go down to South Penhaligon for their service, but we will be back for 6.30pm. By the time you've had a glass or two here we will be back. No mince pies or whisky there for us, it's a 'duty calls' job, I'm afraid. Anyway, got to say bringing Gervaise out of retirement was one of Alex's better ideas. Makes for such a special occasion." Just for once, I found myself wholeheartedly agreeing with her. "We will have nowhere near as much fun down there, but we always go, and so go we must." She separated Alex from his whisky, and off they shot.

I caught sight of Col, tucking into a mince pie. "Evening, Col, how are you?"

"I'm OK. Love the church. It's really special. My two, who are around somewhere, were open mouthed at all the candles." He hesitated. Col hated to share his personal problems, but I could always see a share coming. "One thing. Don't like to mention it, but now Lettice has found the wagon is still going, she has been really quite offhand, and do you know what? She has even started to get a little demanding!"

"Demanding, Col? Lettice? In what way, demanding? Hmmm, do tell." With some men this would be the cue for a stream of ribald remarks, but Col was not one of those men.

"Well, I've seen her twice towards the end of a day's hunting, and she has rather suggested that, as I got such

102

a good deal, perhaps the least I could do is wash her horse off once we have finished. Well, to be honest, as you know I'm a pretty helpful chap." He was a byword for selfless helpfulness, was Col, often to his own detriment, so there was no arguing with this statement. "But, you know, while I would help if I had the time, you being one of the Masters and not finishing till late means the light's going. I've barely got time to do our horses, but she can be really quite sharp."

The poor chap looked really uncomfortable. He was clearly embarrassed, but at a loss how to deal with this awkward situation.

"I do think we had a conversation about this at the time you bought the wagon," I remarked, and immediately regretted the sheer uselessness of the observation. "Look, Col, I'm really sorry. I'm afraid Lettice is like a dog with a bone, she won't give up. It's embarrassing, Col, let me have a think on it. I could talk to her, but that might just encourage her even more to be a little, shall we say, high handed. I do know how unsettling it is for you."

Actually it was more than unsettling. Col depended on the Lettices of this world for his goodwill and reputation; his was a life working with horses, no matter who owned them. When Col took your horse into his care, it became his for the period. The job was never going to make him rich, but it was what he loved and was very good at. Not only was he a decent man himself, he gave others an insight into the fact that decency was a natural way of being. Lettice's bullying behaviour was beginning to make me cross. Col was my friend, and in a difficult position to argue his corner and protect himself from this rather catty and, in my view, slightly abusive behaviour.

However, with Malcolm just five yards away in full flow, now was clearly not the right time to tackle her on the subject.

The drinks party was beginning to disperse. Gervaise, in his role of shepherd, was persuading his flock towards the door, not that a huge amount of persuasion was necessary. The cold of the Blankshire night was beginning to steal into the old building, and overcoats were being pulled tightly around bodies. I wandered out into the night; next stop, Charlotte and Alex.

FOURTEEN

The Final Hurdle

I T WAS ALMOST six in the evening. Although just over a mile to Alex's Big House, I decided to leave the car and walk. A walk on an English winter night such as this, with the first tendrils of frost falling on to the ground, was exactly what I wanted. It had the bonus of helping to walk off the warmth of the whisky, which was just beginning to generate that slight sense of fuzzy logic we call tipsy.

So much sensation to enjoy: frost crunching in the grass; brisk cold on the cheek; white mist of exhalation drifting behind. I walked briskly, savouring the peace and the huge starscape that now inhabited the heavens. Not for Blankshire the pale wan night sky almost occluded by street lighting of the city. Here the various constellations, familiar from childhood, were clear to see.

I crossed the road and went into the park of the Big House. Here the hunt horses lived, together with the fine breeding bulls that were a speciality of the estate. The drive up to the house itself was almost a mile long, and as I neared the end my ears and nose were beginning to tingle. The prospect of warmth tantalised me. Alex's car headlights appeared behind me; the travellers from South Penhaligon were returning.

The window was wound down. "Want a lift?"

"Thanks, Charlotte, but I've made it this far and would rather continue with my Captain Oates moment."

I'd enjoyed my afternoon and wanted to take in the cold night air a little longer. I liked the cold; it made me feel fully alive. Leave the heat of the south for others; no sweaty mosquito-ridden sleep for me, thank you. I'd worked in the tropics at one time, and the British climate, with all its ups and downs, was perfect. And the cold gave me a chance to rehearse what I needed to discuss with Alex and Charlotte. Five minutes later I was at the door, just as they arrived and unlocked it.

Alex had only lost his father very recently, and the house had a still, dank unoccupied feel to it. It was freezing. Charlotte threw a light switch and a single bulb lit up at the far end of the entrance hall. Very little was visible. Unlike the home of William, this entrance hall was not grand; rather the grandeur lay beyond the various doors, now closed and, in all probability, locked. The dimly lit walls were lined with portraits, some of Elizabethan adventurers and piratanical looking coves. That gene had long since vanished.

Alex called me after me, "Sorry it's so cold. Come through to the kitchen. Mum" in fact, the Dowager Lady Susan "has gone to Iberia on a Saga extended winter break. You know, quite extraordinary. Since Dad died, first of all she wouldn't leave the house, convinced as soon as she walked out the door we'd throw her out onto the street, then, once we'd persuaded her everything will still be here when she gets back, she's off on a charabanc for two months. Tea?"

The kitchen was not the Victorian original. It was remarkable only as a piece of utterly threadbare fifties kitsch, apart from the inevitable Aga, chipped and battered, its cream colour long since faded into a variety of grimy hues. However, it did have the merit of being warm. Alex offered me a genuine 1950s stool to perch on, and moved his near to the Aga.

"Thing is, Dad was never exactly liberal with his money. As a family we have learnt to be pretty careful, too many years of rapacious tax demands have taught us that. While they had a good go at this kitchen, ooooh, so many years ago – these units were straight from a Kings Road designer, believe it or not – there was never money to revisit. Of course, as farming improved Dad was always busy. Usually only the staff ever saw this place, and then, as happens to all of us, the vital spark started to fade. Familiar becomes far more important than new, and here we are. Thirty years, I reckon, since this place saw any paint.

"Now there has been quiet civil war. Mum wishes to stay, why I don't know. I'd like to skip a generation and let my youngster and his wife start afresh. Got to say, if you were starting afresh this'd be place to start, eh?" He looked around wistfully. "Of course, the couple who help out in the kitchen and about the house have got old too."

He traced his finger across the Aga top, marvelling at the bow wave of sludge building up as he drew his finger along. "Anyway, didn't invite you up here for a session of all our yesterdays, did we, dear?" Charlotte, who was pouring the tea, smiled and nodded approbation.

This was interesting. It seemed a plan was about to be produced for me, a turn up for the books. I hoped I was going to like what was coming next; if I didn't, I realised there would be no shifting them. Singularly Alex could be stubborn; with Charlotte behind him, he could put a conference of mules to shame.

"Anyway, we've had a good think. Impressed by the effort at William's, it was a good night. Pity about the belted earl rambling on like that, but, like us, he comes with the county, and you've got to put up with him." After a meditative pause, and a gulp at his tea, Alex continued.

"We've been thinking. Talked to the house, of course." I supposed he meant the various retainers who hobbled about the place, leaving beans on toast for the Dowager and walking the dogs when the mood took them, although I rather enjoyed the notion of Alex communing, on bended knees, with the old pile itself. "Yes, anyway, they think it possible, so the house is squared. Of course I have also talked to the trustees and the estate company."

Alex practically owned both of them, so I'd have thought it would have been a short dialogue with himself in front of the bathroom mirror. However nothing, as I had learnt, could ever be that simple.

This conversation, for example, was clearly designed to underpin some act of supreme generosity rather than impart information. I decided humour was not my strong suit in this situation. Listen and don't interrupt generally worked best, and then find point(s) of agreement. I had attempted to exploit the Alex humour vein in the past, but it was shallow and easily exhausted.

"So," Alex carried on, "a consensus seems to be emerging that something can be done. We'll need a committee, of course." In Alex's world, committees existed for him to chair, take credit as appropriate, and distribute blame when others (it was always others) failed. "I was thinking the members should include myself, Charlotte as she is going to have to do a lot of the work, then I thought Lettice…" At this point, he reeled off the names of the ladies from the racquets club. The design was taking shape, but so far he had neglected to illuminate whether this committee would be designing a camel or a horse.

The doorbell rang. Without waiting for it to be answered, in strode Philip Quinn-Harkin, my fellow Joint Master who had, to date, been significant only by his absence of meaningful contribution.

"Charlotte! Alex!" It appeared I was relegated to the role of house ghost. "Evening, you two. I was passing, saw lights on, and thought maybe you were having a drink. Well I'm never one to miss out, eh Alex?" And finally, "Oh, evening, Hector. Nice to see you here too. Something interesting to discuss?"

Alex caught the question and ducked the answering of it rather neatly.

"Yes, well, Philip, nice to see you obviously, but we were just having tea, actually. Bit of a catch up with Hector here, and then we were going to do the Christmas decorations afterwards, but seeing as you're here, tea?"

This was all the excuse Philip needed. He breezed on ingratiatingly about the joys of the carol service, "Not quite sure why we needed candles, electricity is marvellous stuff", the prospects for next day's sport, and generally danced attendance in a rather queasy-making fashion. I was beginning to feel like a bit of a spare part at the court of King Alex. I was many things, but an obsequious retainer was not one of them.

This had gone on for long enough. "Philip, let's cut to the chase. Before you appeared, Alex was explaining the need for a committee, chaired by himself. We were just getting on to the purpose of the committee, so, Alex, put me out of my misery. What exactly are you planning that involves this place? A ball? Vintage car rally perhaps? Going to get some lions like Longleat maybe?" Oops, gone too far. I was beginning to sound like the belted earl, and Alex's response was predictably testy.

"No, don't be ridiculous! It's obvious to me what we need is a grand auction. A proper once in a generation event, one that is capable of raising the whole £35k or whatever it is. Going to kill this one off and sort the stables, improve the assets of the estate into the bargain, and stop that fella having an excuse to wander around my property." We all knew who he meant.

This was most unlike Alex. Normally the most diffident and practically indecisive of men, he clearly had a whole plan of campaign which he was about to unfold.

"What, you're prepared to throw the whole house open?" Shocked at this lurch from genteel unhelpfulness to outright commitment, I realised William's prediction had been closer to the mark than I'd thought at the time. I had been hoping for this outcome, but had not expected it to be served up on a tray with ice and a twist of lemon.

"Well yes, of course. Obviously! How else would we do it? Mum approves. She's quite excited, actually, muttering about it being like the old days. Be the first time in thirty years we've done anything like this. Big undertaking, you know, opening up the ballroom, the large dining room, and the main reception. First things first though, Hector, there are some conditions." Here Charlotte, the detail expert, talked me through the small print.

"Naturally, after all the work you did on the cook book, we'd expect you to help with this." A pointed look. "No" was not a viable option.

Without pausing for so much as a breath, never mind any sign of assent from me, she ploughed on. "And we would expect everyone on the committee to contribute something of real value. In addition all the big landowners must at least match what we are prepared to do, which is a day's shooting at Thrillers Bottom, you know, right at the top end of the estate. Good spot, that, normally fetches about three thousand pounds." She enunciated her words carefully to underscore the significance of what was being offered. "Given there are six or seven of us in the county, that adds up pretty quickly, but, and this is important, we do expect *all* the usuals to contribute." She peered pointedly over her pince-nez at me, and I could guess which particular usual she was focused upon.

"In addition, your task will be to obtain lesser auction lots: days fishing, weekend at someone's flat in London, crate of champagne, that sort of thing. We think you know the fellow travellers, those not like us. Not the sort of people I get around to talking to very often. Anyway, we Bicesters like to do things with a certain style. Make other people wish they'd made the effort. I need to make sure Lettice is on side. She has been a bit stand-offish of late, had you noticed?"

I had. "Would you like me to explain the reason why?"

"Hector, I'm sure whatever trivial matter it is, it's nothing I can't overcome."

Amazing how such stubborn people were capable of underestimating the equal stubbornness of their contemporaries. At least William knew he was difficult. Charlotte, having dealt with Lettice many times over the years, was sure she would easily be persuaded. I was not; not until Lettice had found a way to square Malcolm off, anyway.

"Well?" breezed Charlotte.

"Well, no chance of this thing flying without Lettice," interjected Alex, "so something better be thought of." He looked at me significantly, and having increased my burden moved on. "Now what we don't know is how the belted earl will respond. He's awfully careful with his brass." A wild understatement here, but at least the issue was being pulled, kicking and cowering, out into the open. Had Alex and Charlotte devised a way of solving it for me?

"Without him, I'm afraid we, as a family, do not wish to participate. This really has to be a collective effort from all the people like us. That's how it used to be in the old days.

I'll give you the tour of this place sometime if you like, show you the various ancestors. They're all here, some of his as well as ours. Generations of the blighters!"

"Anyway, our challenge is to find a way around the short arms, deep pockets syndrome. The belted earl never seems to have got over the fortune his pa spent on his hunting, or," Charlotte added waspishly, "perhaps the fact that people liked his pa."

"Bit harsh that, Charlotte," remarked Alex, but then chipped in with his own observation which sounded remarkably similar to me. "But I'm afraid it's true. In my experience, people don't appreciate his particular form of one hundred percent cash management approach. Difficult man to warm to, as you know." So we'd recognised the problem at great length, but still no solutions were on offer. Very helpful!

Philip could stand being left on the sidelines no longer. Practically beside himself with impatience, he wanted to be heard.

"Alex, Charlotte, well I have to say that's awfully good of you. Grand auction, that will get the whole county bouncing up and down. Able to come to the Big House, too. How good that will be?" Ruddy face aglow, Philip rubbed his hands together like an insanely enthusiastic butcher about to retrieve the favourite side of steak for his best customer. "Awfully good it'll be. 'Course, I'm only too pleased to help any way I can."

Charlotte stared at him for a few seconds, then decided to bow to the inevitable. "Of course, Philip, in your capacity as Joint Master it does make sense if you are on the organising committee too. If you're prepared to and you really think it will help, that is?"

"Delighted, Charlotte, delighted! Can't have Hector taking the credit for all the bright ideas around here, can we?

Indeed, I know the earl, Sid actually, pretty well, I think. Not such a bad fellow." Philip didn't seem to have caught the mood of the hanging jury. I watched Alex's face lengthen.

"Well someone will need to tackle the fellow on the subject," he pointed out.

Philip, incorrigible now in front of people he always wanted to impress, leapt in and grabbed the challenge. "And do you know what? As we're going full steam ahead I think I'm just the man, Alex? I reckon I'll get some change out of the old skinflint. What do you think?" Another crazed bout of hand rubbing followed this brave declaration of intent. Alex frowned; *lèse majesté* was never to be encouraged, even if it referred to his much frowned upon rival, as once started it had a habit of not stopping. In his mind it was a small step from this to the downfall of Charles I, and in the Bicester household this was considered a comparatively recent domestic tragedy.

"Philip, if it is the earl you're referring to, I think your suggestion to approach him discreetly and invite an early contribution is most welcome. Thank you. As you know, he and I don't always see eye to eye, and a properly couched word from you could conceivably do the trick. I wouldn't fancy having to approach him myself. Nothing he enjoys more than being awkward and rude, and saying 'No' to me. It would be like having an extra Christmas Day for him, but if you want to have a go..."

"Don't you worry, Alex, you know me." Clearly we did, and that was what worried us. "I know the fellow pretty well. Sure I'll be able to talk him into something for the greater good." As always, Philip was the relentless optimist – often to the bitter end.

For my part, I was quietly pleased that the first assault on Castle Belted Earl would involve someone other than me knocking at the seldom breached front door. I had little hope that it would produce the right result, but it was only proper to ask before flying in reinforcements for the approach I was planning. This way the earl would have been warned, and the court of public opinion would already be lined up against him.

For now, we discussed the finer details at some length. I prevailed upon our little company to keep quiet, at least until we had talked to Lettice and possibly the earl. While a major piece of the jigsaw was now in place, I was concerned that Lettice still remained outside our tent.

FIFTEEN

Splash

O N BOXING DAY we met at eleven in the Market Square at Upper Malsham. This was what we always did, and I had little doubt the ancestors had done it too. Today there was a big crowd of spectators. I discovered Col, with his new lorry parked alongside that of Letttice. Being slightly behind schedule I quickly climbed on Michael and headed for the Market Square. Turning the corner, a rousing sight appeared in front of me: over a hundred horses, many decorated with tinsel for a very festive effect.

I saw Lettice and coaxed Michael through the mounted throng towards her. "Morning Lettice, George." Her young son, George, almost as dashing as his father, was by her side. I knew Charlotte had planned to talk to Lettice in reasonable, measured and sensible tones, but this was obviously going to fail, so the thorny problem of squaring her off remained.

Fortunately Lettice had a different preoccupation. "Taking the new lorry tomorrow. It's the big race for Jumbo Hill, the best racehorse Malcolm has ever owned, at Kelso you know. That's a 600 mile round trip, and will take the groom nearly eight hours to drive, even in the new lorry, so we're going to have to be getting back today reasonably early. It'll be the biggest day of the year for Malcolm, so I need to make sure he enjoys every second of it. I'm rather excited,

Hector. All the pundits say it's in with a good chance, so Malcolm's got a quick horse and a slow, dependable lady." She grinned foolishly.

As always with Lettice's quirkier observations, I felt it best to duck and move quickly on. "Have you talked to Charlotte at all?" I queried tentatively, curious to put my theory that Lettice was seriously out of sorts about the wretched lorry business to the test. "She was muttering to me about a grand auction."

"Yes, she did say something about that. Thing is, you know, I'm sure I do more than enough, and at the moment I'm rather walking on eggshells around Malcolm. Can't be too careful. If he finds out about the lorry business there could be hell to pay, and he already thinks we're a bit of a rabble."

That rather confirmed my theory. Lettice first, second, and third; the rest, nowhere. Now was clearly not the time for a real go. At that moment the huntsman, Anthony blew a long sonorous note on his horn, largely to impress the spectators, then he and his hounds set off for the annual visitation around Upper Malsham. We received rousing cheers as hounds were paraded around, and then we headed, to the sound of the hunting horn, for the green fields and wooded countryside where we belonged.

Boxing Day had many traditions associated with it. It was a day for the gaudy dressing up of the horses, for trotting by the three old peoples' homes, and then a further pit stop down at Lower Malsham. Another tradition was that it wasn't really a day for hunting at all. Too many wildly over-excited novices and too many horses. For the first two hours or so, all of the traditions were observed to the letter. A lot of idling around and casual chatter; riding from A to B and then back again via C; fruitless activity by the hounds in places where no self respecting fox had been found in decades. By two o'clock most of the once a year field, the happy hackers, had slipped quietly away. We were now down to the regulars, and turned on to the riverbank itself. Here there were possibilities. The weather had been good, way too good for the stalwarts, the light bright and airy with an unseasonable touch of warmth in the air, but now rain clouds appeared, scudding low and angry. As time moved on, the light started to change. Shadows appeared and, although there were still two hours of daylight left, the day was well beyond middle age and fading rapidly.

At the same time the temperature was dropping. This augured well for a little sport; typically it was much easier to follow the trail if the weather was colder.

We had been following the riverbank for an hour now, and would soon start a long slow turn for home. Lettice had appeared again. Glancing at the sky, she commented, as only Lettice would, "Well, if it starts to rain and my knickers get wet" she grinned at me "I'm going home." As it turned out her remark would be remarkably prescient, although not in a way any of us imagined. She then carried on chatting happily about the wretched Jumbo Hill and what a triumph it would be if he won at Kelso. Even my patience was being tested.

Suddenly from a small patch of gorse, almost beneath the feet of the horses, a great, big dog fox stood up, shook himself, and decided that hiding was no longer for him. There was a cry and a holler from one of our mounted number to alert the huntsman and hounds, who had now nearly passed on. The fox shot off, and, hearing the cry of the hounds behind him, decided rather imaginatively to swim for it. There was a splash as he slid into the river, then a ruddy head appeared doggy paddling vigorously away to the far bank. A nimble and fit fox can swim well, even though the river at that point was some fifty feet wide. The dog fox climbed on to the far bank, and had a quick shake and a look around. As he did so the hounds, nothing daunted, followed his trail to the water's edge, the leading hounds arriving just in time to see our friend toddle confidently away, satisfied his brush was now safe. This was seen by the lead hound as an outrageous provocation. Giving tongue, a great strangled cry of canine anguish, he leapt. There was a huge splash as sixty pounds of frustrated hound landed in the river, then he surfaced, paddling strongly for the other side. The rest quickly followed, splash, splosh, splash, and within seconds there were thirty-seven creatures doggy paddling frantically away. Then the young huntsman, Anthony, swoon handsome in his red coat, galloped up to me.

"Want me to go with them, sir, or call them back?"

I glanced at the river. It was just about doable, and we had not done much today. A bit of excitement was clearly called for. "Your horse swims, doesn't it, Anthony?"

"Only one way to find out, sir,"

As the pack of hounds splashed across the river, the music of their cry continuing even as they breasted the current, Anthony turned his horse to the water, and I followed. Of course horses can swim, out of need or obedience, but on a cold winter's day they are not over keen. I knew the feeling. Michael needed encouragement but go he did, the water rising in a great bow wave in front of him, the current tugging at both of us. The water grew deeper, rising to my boots – oh – then ouch – into my boots. Michael kicked, and briefly we were swimming. I leant forward to lower my centre of gravity, but this was the tricky bit. I had never been on a capsizing horse, and didn't want to be on one now. The water was soaking into my coat, into my groin – ouch, that was bloody cold. I'd never thought of myself as a shrinking violet, but parts of me were now. With another powerful kick, and three more strides of swimming I felt my horse's feet touch land again. He struggled briefly to regain his footing, another great surge and splash, and a heave of equine power saw him rising from the river. There was a mad scramble of legs onto river bank, water rushing off us both, then a great shake from my horse. I stood in the stirrups and gave him as much freedom as possible as he endeavoured to rid himself of the icy wetness.

Ahead of us the hounds streamed, not in the slightest bit perturbed by their swim. Behind me the more intrepid members of the field followed. There was a loose horse swimming riderless, and a great shriek of laughter from Mrs Forbes Beresford, not a day under seventy, splashing across with her horse. "Aahhhh", Sploshaassshhhhh! Ginger, a corpulent sort of chap, toppled as his horse launched into a sideways crawl. Now forced to use his abundant girth as a flotation device, he was swimming frantically. Separated totally from his horse, one was heading towards this bank, the other to the other.

Lettice was just behind me, urging her horse on, the pressure of time and the need to be somewhere else forgotten. Her boy, George, was on his small pony next to her, kicking off, swimming madly, boy soaked, horse soaked, but completely engaged by the excitement of the moment.

I looked ahead. The huntsman, Anthony, was half a field in front of me, up just behind the hounds. I pushed Michael on; truthfully in these situations he needed little pushing, willingly he responded. He knew his job now: to keep up and see this onwards to wherever it would lead. Ahead of us the hounds streamed over a small stone wall. Anthony and his horse hesitated for a second, then sprang over. I followed quickly behind. There were now only a dozen or so horses left with us; the remainder had elected tamely to wait on the far river bank and see the outcome. Fortune favours the brave, and it would only be those who'd crossed the river who would experience the next part of the adventure. We were now galloping into the country of our neighbours landscape without familiar landmarks. The only point of reference was the sound of the hounds in front, one moment closing up, the next receding from us, depending upon the vagaries of the fox.

As we galloped, the wind cold and fresh in our faces, I moved alongside Anthony. His eyes were lit up with excitement.

"Proper job, sir. What do you say?"

"Keep on, Anthony. Your job, not mine."

In front of us was a serious obstacle: a wire fence to hurdle. Normally we'd stop or look for a gate, but this time the pace was too fast. Kick on, kick on! I remembered my lessons, aiming at a fence post. Anthony's horse flew over the wire; mine obediently following, mimicking the herd leader. Now there were only six of us; those born with sense had pulled up at the wire. A small hedge, easily hurdled, and we were into a field full of root vegetables. As we landed it was clear the hounds had lost their scent. They milled around, searching, anxiously looking up to Anthony for guidance. He blew a short note on his horn and moved beyond the vegetables where, for whatever reason, evidence of the fox still lay. The hounds burst into their full cry, like a steam engine at full tilt. "Here he is, here he is, here he is," they seemed to be saying, rhythmic and compelling. A narrative that had to be followed; a narrative as old as human history. Heads down again, we were charging after the rediscovered scent, horses panting but still keen, the river bank a good mile and a half behind us. Through an open gateway, into a long grass field, hounds running quickly, horses straining to keep up, riders oblivious to anything other than the excitement. Thoughts of cold legs and wet feet were not yet intruding. A small jump took us into a further grass field and the beginnings of the low hills that marked where the higher ground began. Still the hounds ran on, but slower now. Clearly the pace was telling on all the participants. A glance back showed the same half a dozen riders left, including Lettice and her George; the rest of the field had fallen behind us.

A large post and rail fence presented itself. Sitting back, nerves tingling, apprehension in the stomach; please, God, let the horse jump this. As good as gold, Michael bounced, big and free. The momentary sensation of heavenly weightlessness, and then a neat landing on the far side followed by a great slapping pat on the horse's neck. "Good lad, well done!" The horse was alive with adrenalin, wanting to be on with the hounds.

And then, as quickly as the fast thing had started, it petered out. Almost five miles from the crossing point of the river the scent had faded away to nothing. Anthony went around the last point where the hounds had made a noise, casting in big circles, then between gasps confirmed my suspicions.

"Afraid we are gonna to have to give this 'un best, sir. We've lost 'im. No idea where the beggar has got to. Those sheep over there, he'll have slinked round 'em a few times, and now all we can sniff is the smell of 'em and not 'im." I think he meant the fox was gone. "Been a good run though, sir," he added.

"I know, Anthony. Well done, you. In the meantime, small detail. Any idea where we are?"

I glanced at my watch. It was now almost 3.30 and the light was fading. We were clearly not going to get back the way we had come in the daylight left to us.

"To be honest, sir, not really. Not our patch, is it?"

"OK, let's take the hounds over there to the road, and I'll see if I can find someone around to call the wagons over here."

Lettice and her son caught us up.

"Anthony, that was absolutely thrilling, but how am I going to get home from here? I've come way further than I intended."

Resisting the temptation to point out this question belonged in the past and not the present, I had a think.

"Look, let's get to the road, find a car follower, and you and George can go back with them to get the lorries. Let Colin know I'm here, and you can come back for the horses and the hounds in your wagon, but please can we crack on." I was beginning to feel the biting easterly breeze, and I needed warmth. My toes were rapidly turning to ice.

"Yes, yes, you're quite right." We hacked briskly with the hounds to the road, found a car follower, and posted Lettice and George back towards Little Barff where the lorries would be waiting. Then we stood, holding the horses while the hounds paced the verge close by, great tongues lolling as they recovered from their exertions. We waited, and we waited. In this part of Blankshire there was little in the way of traffic. A tractor and its trailer, loaded with turnips, headlights dimmed, rattled by, its driver giving us a friendly wave. We jogged our horses in circles; I ran my hands under my horse's saddle in a fruitless effort to keep them warm. Time ticked by, and the body thermometer fell. This was not good.

Finally, in the distance I heard the grind of lorries, and headlights were appearing in the gloaming. The Blankshire hunt lorry appeared first, then came the lorry of Mrs Forbes Beresford. Col brought up the rear; well, I thought, three lorries would be enough. Then I realised Lettice was sitting in the lorry with Col. Her shoulders were heaving, and it looked as though she was in tears.

Something had clearly gone wrong.

SIXTEEN

Turnips

J UST FOR ONCE, Lettice and her drama were going to have to play second fiddle. My toes were losing their battle with the cold, and I rather wanted them to remain on the ends of my feet, so as Col clambered from the lorry I went to the passenger side.

"Budge over, Lettice, I'm coming in. I need warmth, and badly." My fingers had turned a particularly unhealthy shade of blue. I climbed into the wagon, and said a small prayer of thanks for the fact the lorry heater worked.

As Lettice shifted over I began to feel for the heater. I had far too many wet and nearly frozen clothes on for the change in external temperature to do me much good. Hell, what next? Losing clothes and donning something, anything, not wet was my priority, but at that moment a keening sob emerged from Lettice, perched beside me.

"Hector, Hector, the wagon, the wagon." This seemed to be the gist of the low moaning as she rocked backwards and forward, sucking at small pink fingers, but at this point all I could think of was removing the two blocks of ice that used to be my hunting boots.

"Lettice, I'm sorry. At this precise moment I'm really not interested in your wagon. Please, please help me pull these boots off while I still have a complete set of toes. Please!"

Lettice released a further teary groan, but began to focus on my predicament. I had no doubt a similar scene was being enacted in the hunt lorry. It was cold and it was late, and we needed to get out of these wet clothes quickly. Lettice seemed to grasp there were other people on earth outside her upset self and set to with a will, grabbing a boot.

"For God's sake, Hector, undo your bloody garter straps, otherwise I'll never get them off."

Through gritted teeth I cursed myself. "Sorry, Lettice, can you do it? Fingers utterly gone."

As I struggled with numb fingers to undo the strap that went round my calf top and kept the top of the boot secure, Lettice helped out with this slightly intimate act and suddenly grinned at me through her misery.

"Tell you what, you'll know pain when the circulation returns."

Bloody woman. That was not what I wanted to hear! She tugged and pulled at my boot, and suddenly it popped – no, slithered – free. The same treatment for the other one, and then the wet and dripping socks were removed. Finally my poor, cold feet emerged, bone white and almost without sensation. Holding them up to the heater…phew…

"Lettice, it's alright for you. You've changed already. Rummage in the back for me and see if you can find my overcoat." It was the only item of dry clothing I possessed at this moment.

She did this obligingly as I slid my partially sodden red hunt coat off, then my shirt and undershirt. I quickly donned the overcoat; thinly but dryly clad now, at least I was partially able to dry out. As I did so, the real Lettice suddenly re-emerged. Tears shaken away, now Lettice meant her own form of business again.

"Look, Hector, you know it's not like me to cry, but

I've had a really horrid accident. Nearly wrecked the new wagon. What am I going to do? Turnips, bloody turnips everywhere. Never seen anything like it. Came round the corner, and there was a bloody turnip tractor. I was in such a hurry – crash! A bit of ice on the road, and there wasn't time. I was going too fast...bang! Crash! It was scary, honestly. Lucky I had my seat belt on, but I wacked into the back of the bloody trailer. My shiny, new box: the radiator has popped, and the road is full of turnips, all exploded and squashed. It's the big race tomorrow, and now I'm stuck. How am I going to tell Malcolm?"

Not the most coherent account. It sounded like a film run at high speed, the images a bit jumbled, but I had the gist. Stifling a grin at the thought of turnips a leaping and cavorting everywhere, I decided to be practical.

"Lettice, let me get this clear. What you're really telling me is, histrionics aside, you need to produce a horse transporter in the next thirty minutes to get you, the groom, the wretched Jumbo Hill, and Malcolm to Kelso?"

"Well yes, obviously, and now you're dry you can be a little more polite, please. And, if you don't mind, we're going in the Range Rover not the lorry, but I do need to find a lorry. We're miles from any phone. It's hopeless. Malcolm can be sooo difficult, and this could be very awkward for me, Hector." She gazed at me, and I saw the real fright on her face. The chasm was opening up before her, and her resolve was clearly wavering.

I rather like a crisis, particularly when it belongs to someone else. I can be rather inventive, and this one was perfect.

"Lettice, don't you remember? Didn't you agree with Colin when you sold him the wagon that if he managed to get it going again, it could act as an emergency back up to you and your lovely new lorry? You know, almost like having him on call as it were? I cannot think of a better time to call than now, can you?"

"Did I agree to that?"

"Well, to be honest, Lettice, I dunno. I wasn't there, was I? But I reckon if any of us had suggested it at the time you would have agreed to it, and so would he. That's very nearly the same thing."

Now, I thought, let's turn the dagger a little. "But you're going to have to turn on the famous Lettice charm for Colin. No more suggesting that he washes your horse off after a long and tiring day, or making him feel he needs to hide his wagon round the corner just to save your blushes."

"They were only supposed to be jokes. Maybe not my better jokes," she said unconvincingly.

"Well a joke to you maybe, but it's not always so funny to him, and we can't unjoke them, can we? He was really quite offended. Look, tell you what, I'll ask the hunt staff to take my horse back to the stables and if – and it's a big if, Lettice – we both speak respectfully to Colin, make him feel like one of us, I think he will respond well. You may just get your lend/lease lorry. Also, I reckon, when you get back home and Malcolm starts shouting the odds, wanting to know what's going on, Colin can suddenly appear like a Jack-in-a-box with the solution. That'll calm the storm – I can imagine the language otherwise."

"Hector, you don't know him, that might not be enough. Malcolm can be very shouty."

"Not in front of guests who are saving his bacon, Lettice. He's far too well bred, just like you!" I grinned at her; she didn't buy my flattery for a minute, but she smiled. An "any port in a storm" sort of smile, was my diagnosis.

"After all, Malcolm will assume polite face for Colin, and once Colin has explained the arrangement I think his annoyance will be far outweighed by the relief of knowing

Jumbo Hill is practically on his way to Kelso. That, and the relief his darling Lettice and his son and heir are both safe, of course. I'll bet Malcolm's insured up to the eyeballs. He'll like making a claim, and the fact you delivered the solution is going to make him think you're marvellous.

"Now, would you like me to go and ask Colin nicely? Or, on second thoughts, Lettice, you go and talk to him. He's your saviour, not mine. Anyway, I'm not wearing a lot more than this overcoat."

"Hector, you know, I quite agree. Thank you. That's very clear sighted of you. Yes, you're right, I'll speak to Colin. I'll make things right between us." Here she raised an eyebrow at me. "And if I stay in this steamed up wagon with you for much longer, people'll talk. I'm not having that without good reason, I can tell you." She grinned and shot off. Yes, Lettice was back. Before she went, though, one last thought occurred to me.

"Oh, Lettice, Col will need some money for mileage. Thirty-five pence a mile will be about right, cover his depreciation on the wagon and stuff. Persuasive stuff, money."

"Thirty-five pence a mile? Why, that's £200 or more. Even Dick Turpin wore a mask…"

I raised an eyebrow. "It's a commercial world, Lettice. I don't remember ever seeing Colin as a charity…"

"But it's daylight bleeding robbery…"

"It's well past daylight, Lettice. Perilously close to midnight for you, and the clock's ticking." I paused; she could be terribly mean. "Come on! You know and I know Malcolm earns pots of money doing his thing in the city, and don't forget what that horse means to him."

"Yes, I s'ppose." Then her face lit up. "Of course! Colin has always been uncommonly helpful. Such a decent man. When old Russell had that terrible fall Colin was the first to help. Yes, I think I can see your point. And," she added with

127

a grin, "I do keep the farm books, so Malcolm probably won't notice anyway. It's a lot of money, though, Hector."

"Lettice, stop it! Get on, please, put the world to rights. You know you're very good at it."

"OK, OK, I am doing." Now I was winning. Lettice was focusing on how to get her own way again, so I prompted her.

"That's the spirit. Nothing here that can't be put right with a bit of swallowed pride, and we've had a hell of a run today. Just think how excited Malcolm will be when you tell him." Knowing Malcolm I suspected he'd be singularly unimpressed, but Lettice needed a little encouragement.

"Yup, quite right. A proper do it was. Of course, he won't be impressed. You know that, Hector, but that's not the point. This is my fun. I support him with that silly racehorse of his, he can jolly well support me with what I like doing. You're quite right, good for you." The return of Boadicea, and rather nice to have the old girl back.

"And I'm sure I'll persuade Colin. I was a bit beastly to him, I'm afraid, but I was worried."

I was on a roll now. After the exhilaration of the gallop, Lettice had regained her sense of mission. Thoughts of the crashed lorry, drowning in a sea of turnips, were temporarily forgotten, and she just needed a bit of guidance from ground control.

"By the way, Lettice, before you go, I've been meaning to mention…"

She smiled softly at me. Quick, I thought, this women needs little encouragement, just one more favour then I'd quit.

"While we are on the subject, how long have you known Charlotte?"

"I...er...well..." Perhaps not the question she was expecting, but never mind. "Well, Hector, if that's all you want to ask of me, her mum is my aunt. So it must be...well, since we were little girls. Forever, really."

"Well, this grand auction idea. Have you any idea how much effort and thought she has put into it? Can you imagine how many conversations it'll have taken to get Alex out of his normal rut of masterly indecisiveness and persuade him to open up the Big House? You know how vague he can be."

"Vague? Ha, he's practically dead from the neck up!"

"Lettice, that is not true or helpful. He just doesn't find decision making easy, that's all."

"Amazed he can decide to get out of bed some mornings," was the tart rejoiner.

"Lettice! I'm trying to make a point here, if you don't mind."

"Sorry. Still got the adrenalin going, and I do find Alex a bit indecisive. Lovely man, though. You're quite right to tell me off."

"Anyway, why don't you let Charlotte explain again, and see if you and Malcolm can help? I know the shooting on your estate belongs to Malcolm, and he doesn't give much away for nothing. However, I would have thought, when you consider you're transporting Jumbo Hill for him despite the tractor stopping abruptly on that skiddy bit when you were following so gently, he can only admire your ingenuity. I reckon you'll be well placed to persuade him, what d'you think?"

Lettice brightened. "Well, mmm, yes..." Then her grin appeared. "We are going to London shortly. It's our anniversary, and if I'm very nice to him, you know, right underwear and everything..." She smiled at me coquettishly. "Leave it to me."

She suddenly reached out and squeezed my hand. This was not in the script, and I had no desire to help rehearse the re-seduction of Malcolm. I shivered and sneezed, conscious I was wearing little more than an overcoat, and thought quickly.

"You're dry, Lettice. How's Colin getting on with the horses?"

"Oops!" She blushed slightly. "Sorry, mind elsewhere. Forgot myself. Yes, anyway, sorry Hector. I was just...I'll go and see if Colin needs a hand. It might be the perfect opportunity for me to make my peace too with your right good idea."

She opened the door, slithered her backside briefly across the seat, and vanished into the black night. I reached for the thermos, added a huge shot of whisky, and awaited the pain of returning circulation.

Five agonising minutes later, Colin stuck his head into the cab. "Found some trousers for you, boss. Wouldn't want Lettice getting ideas." He had no idea! "Anyway, sudden change of plan. Lettice has asked me a big favour. Been very civil too. Don't know what you said to her, but she seems to be back to normal. So if you wouldn't mind hopping out here you can get a lift back with the hunt servants, and this old wagon is gonna make a mercy dash for Lettice. You'll never believe the mileage rate she's offered me! It'll keep Mrs C smiling. A proper good turn, this is."

SEVENTEEN

Artichoke

THE AFTERMATH OF the turnip lorry incident was relayed back to me via Col. He and Lettice had arrived at Lettice Central to find Malcolm stomping around outside, drawn no doubt by the sound of the blown exhaust recognised from the recent past. The sight of the old lorry he thought had been sent to the knacker's yard only exacerbated his impatience at the late start for Kelso.

His first demand was to discover how "That bloody lorry had come back from the grave?" It appeared the word "bloody" featured frequently as he harangued Lettice, who had been driving. It was only when Col climbed down from the passenger seat that Malcolm reined himself in and actually began to listen. As Col, in his charming and sincere way, explained, Malcolm's fury began to subside.

"My brother worked incredibly hard. At it all hours, he was. Probably spent more than the damn thing's worth, but he owed me a big favour. Reckon I owe him now, but I think it was just worth it. We scraped it through the MOT. Quite remarkable." In his inimitable fashion, Col went on to explain how incredibly lucky it had been that he had bought the wagon, the cleverness of Lettice at having negotiated her "on call" option, and generally dragging her away from danger. An air of constructive calm descended.

Grabbing the moment, Lettice scurried away to get the horses off the wagon and George into a hot bath. By the time she had reappeared, Malcolm was a picture of relieved paternal concern. His only interests now were thanking Col for his trouble, trying to pour a stiff whisky down his neck, and ensuring he had a lift back to Upper Malsham, while a groom loaded Jumbo Hill on to the graveyard lorry, only slightly behind schedule.

So it appeared, from Col's account, that fences had been mended, and Lettice now had room to manoeuvre.

Confirmation came a couple of days later: a postcard from Lettice.

> *Hector,*
> *On call wagon saved the day, brilliant idea. Great time at Kelso. Jumbo Hill finished second, excellent, thanks for all your help. Ref auction, Malc says yes provided 'all others' contribute equally. Fur coat etc not needed! Amazing!!!!!!*
> *Love, L x*

Again back to "all others". I was familiar with the code.

The big challenge now was to talk to the belted earl. I had recently had a phone call from Philip Quinn-Harkin, and his tale had followed sorry but wholly expected lines.

"Hector, Philip here. Up the belted earl's last night. Cocktail party. Great to be invited, actually. Thought to meself, no time like the present. He does a good bash, you know. Anyway, we got to yapping, and naturally I knew it was up to me to charm the auction gift out of him. So I set off, best of intentions.

"By the way, you wouldn't describe me as someone whose parents were obviously not married, would you?"

"I'm sorry, Philip, I'm not sure I'm following you."

"Well, don't worry. We'll come on to that in a minute. Anyway, we did all the usual bits, about his horses. He's cock a hoop his young three-year-old had just beaten Jumbo Hill at Kelso."

What a small world, I thought.

"Anyway, we got on to the subject of the auction. 'Course, he knew all about it. Wanted to hear how it was all going, very pleased to hear others were contributing. Then, just as I was positioning myself, he suddenly excused himself. 'Little matter to deal with,' he said. One minute he was there, next he wasn't. I was left, mouth flapping open, feeling like an idiot. Really didn't appreciate that at all. Anyway, he returned two minutes later with a map of the UK. Quite a big map, in fairness. 'Look at this,' he said, poking at it. 'When my dad succeeded to the title, back in the late thirties, do you know how much of this map my family owned?' "Well, of course I didn't. Why should I? Anyway, he started getting quite emotional. Fair bit of the map, apparently. You know, outlying bits, chunks of Scotland, good bit in the centre of Ireland. All the stuff in some hideous puce colour was theirs. So I had to make appropriate noises of admiration, quite a lot of puce I have to say. Over 220,000 acres in all, he told me. The upshot was that now they are down to 'just 14,000 acres', and only 150 of those are in central London!

"I didn't exactly feel my heart go out to him, but it was quite an impressive thing. He got rather moved by his own eloquence. Half the room had stopped to listen by this stage. He started to get quite heated, and it was awkward I can tell you. Apparently, this land was all lost because his dad, no longer his 'dear old dad' I noticed, had thought of nothing but hunting, morning, noon, and night. I tried to suggest that perhaps 'Dad' had simply enjoyed an appropriate work/life balance, but that just made matters worse. He was having none of it. Practically frothing now, I'll tell you, he didn't look well. Face the same colour as the wretched puce bits on the map.

"That was when he told me I must be a stupid illegitimate so-and-so if I thought we had any chance of persuading him to throw some 'good quality cash' at us, after all his old man had flushed down the khazi. And that's exactly what he said. I'm not making that up, although I was quite surprised at his turn of phase. Wished I hadn't got him so upset," concluded Philip, rather anti-climatically in view of the volcanic eruption of emotions he had exposed himself to.

I reckoned that conversation would have left Philip with scars to the psyche that would probably take years and perhaps therapy to recover from. He was not used to being savaged by people he, from instinct and training, looked up to. In listening it occurred to me that Philip, for all his salesmanship and enthusiasm, could perhaps be a bit slow on the uptake.

Events had pretty well followed the course I had anticipated. It was now time for low cunning and greed to do the work which reason had so significantly failed to accomplish. The necessary opportunity presented itself a couple of days later. As the leading hunt in the area we, the Joint Masters and the Chairman of the Blankshire, were asked from time to time to visit neighbouring hunts to ensure best practice was being followed by those with rather less resources. In essence, this meant a wander round the kennels where the hounds lived, making sure they were looking well, and some general chitchat about our own little world, followed, inevitably, by a convivial lunch and drinks all round. The little working party therefore consisted of the chairman, myself on behalf of the Masters, and, for reasons that had never been explained, William.

I met with William at his Big House and jumped into his pick-up, then we drove over to collect the belted earl. The great man was waiting outside his front door; clearly a man of impeccable timekeeping, he expected the same from us. I jumped into the back seat to leave the front seat to him; it felt easier that way.

The belted earl didn't mention his explosive conversation with Philip, and I had no intention of raising it, not at this stage anyway. As we left the main drive, a mile or so below the earl's generous but not palatial Big House, we approached a tall stone pillar on our right. I had never stopped to inspect it; never really paid it a lot of notice. It was no doubt a monument to some long forgotten ancestor, probably much better loved and remembered in death than in life. They could be terrible brutes some of these self made eighteenth and nineteenth century landowners. The pillar was surmounted by a semicircular object, topped around its perimeter with jagged edges that caught the eye because they were covered in bright, bright, shiniest gold leaf. As we drove towards it, the morning sun flashed from the gold. It clearly caught William's eye, and he winked at me in the rear-view mirror.

"Sid," enquired William, using the belted earl's very familiar name, "I've always been meaning to ask, why have you got a half eaten artichoke on that pillar? See you've had it done out in good style, all that gold leaf. You know, I'd go as far as to say it's the smartest half eaten artichoke I've ever seen!"

"Sorry?" the earl grunted, taken aback by this rather surreal sounding question. "Sorry, not following you at all."

William seized his moment, he was only going to get one go at this. "The thing up there. Every time I drive past with Sally, I say to her, 'You know, darling, frightfully smart, that artichoke. Wonder if we should have one too. I mean, what is the modern country house without a half eaten golden artichoke on a pillar at the end of the drive?"

The earl was grumpy now, and on his mettle. Not angry; more puzzled at William's apparent stupidity. "William, why on earth do you think it'd be an artichoke?"

Another wink from William to me. "Well apart from the fact I can think of nothing it more resembles? I thought, yer know, the Constable-Stricklands introduced the turkey to the UK, and as a result they have a huge bloody great turkey on their coat of arms. We used to do a lot of messin' about in boats, so we have a rather splendid racing yacht on ours. I'd assumed an ancient but significant claim to fame of your lot was the introduction of the artichoke. I thought I'd worked that bit out, feeling rather pleased with myself actually, I was just mystified by the symbolism of it being half eaten..."

This was too much for the choleric belted earl. "Look, it is NOT an artichoke. As any fool would know, it's a cauldron of flame symbolising the light and warmth the fifth earl brought into the world. Half eaten artichoke, indeed. Preposterous."

"Steady on, old man, I was only asking. Terribly sorry, clearly got that a bit wrong. Never mind. Our lot imported great yachts, and I thought maybe your lot did marvellous artichokes. Not an unreasonable assumption, don't ya think?"

"No, I bloody well don't! It's not a sodding artichoke, it's a cauldron. Do you realise how much money I've spent renewing the gold leaf? And now you're suggesting it looks like a ruddy half eaten artichoke. God, I knew your father, and I thought he was pretty bloody...huummphh."

Here civility assaulted anger and knocked it to the ground. Restraint assumed control of a situation that had threatened to spin out of any tethered orbit. The ricochet could have been dangerous, and already there were casualties, including the earl's facial expression. Boot faced and tight lipped, he had nothing nice to say and realised that not saying it was the best course of action. Inevitably, conversation in his present mood was only going to further his reputation for incivility, at least so his bulging veins and clamped jaw suggested.

The silence edged into time, and judging by the silly grin on William's face he was content simply to enjoy the moment. He gazed beatifically into the middle distance, replaying his silly nonsense, and savouring every syllable of its absurdity. I didn't blame him, and suspected I had been in at the genesis of a tale that would grow in the telling. I also thought it would suit me as the earl would, in my estimation, now be keen to find a sympathetic ear.

The temperature in the car had hardly risen as we arrived at the kennels of the Malsham Harriers, a foot pack based on the far side of Malsham. We wandered around, and I got the opportunity to chat to the earl.

"It's the shooting day coming up soon. Looking forward to it?"

"Well yes, of course. Great family tradition for the Bicesters and ourselves. I get to tease old Alex no end, always rather enjoy it. Get to look around his place too. Chance to remind myself how much better organised we…" Realising he was about to be indiscreet, he went quiet.

"Good shot, is he? Lord Blankshire, I mean."

"Alex? Well yes, he does his best, doesn't he? By most people's standards I'd say he is pretty good, but we belted earls like to play to the top of our game. And when we are there, we take some beating…"

Ah, the traps vanity leads otherwise sensible men into!

"So, you'd say you could outshoot Alex, would you?"

"Well…" After the episode with William in the car, the belted earl was keen to demonstrate he was all calm and self-assured. "Obviously, old boy, modesty prevents me from saying too much."

"I was thinking, how about a little wager between us consenting adults? It might get us all out of a tight spot."

"A wager, you say?" He glanced at me with a gleam of interest in his reptilian eyes.

"Yes. You and Alex. You win if you outshoot him on the shooting day, he wins if the scores are even. Your head keeper and his to keep score. D'you think we can trust them to do that?"

"But, of course! Sound chaps those keepers. Both been with us for years."

"The stake money will be a day's shooting at your place next season, generously given by you for the auction, including lunch and dinner, all hosted by you, plus a £2,000 donation on top. That should get people's attention." In for a penny, I thought. It would be a pretty tidy sum for one or other of us to drop. "If you win, I'll underwrite the cost, so one way or another you maintain your reputation" and here I pushed my luck "for being a benefactor whose generosity is often remarked upon..." I left the sentence vague and unfinished, quietly enjoying the ambiguity. "Given your talent, sounds to me like you could afford to give Alex a bit of a handicap, say credit him with ten birds up before the fun begins?"

"Calm down. I never said anything about giving away an advantage. Never said he was a bad shot, either. If that's the wager, and the odds are practically fifty-fifty, I say let the better man win."

He bit hard on the bait, lured into a firm commitment by dismissing my suggestion of the additional handicap, and so his greed effectively closed the sale for me. Now we weren't discussing whether he should, but the best terms on which he would engage.

He proffered a hand, and we shook on the deal. Now I had a phone call to make. Albert had better be there when I needed him.

*

I caught Albert a day or so later, as ever rushing around, and launched into a long explanation about how my plan would be good for his business, give him exposure to Blankshire's aristos, help increase awareness and his reputation no end. I was allowed to witter for a good five minutes with little coming back the other way.

Finally a grunt. "You finished, mister?"

"I'm sorry, Albert, have I not made myself plain?"

"You've made yerself plain as a pikestaff. You're in trouble, and yer want my help to get you out. Is that not correct, 'Ector?"

"Well...umm, well...ummm...yes," I blustered. "I suppose, if you put it in those terms, can't think of a better person than you to..."

Albert interrupted. "Look, 'Ector, I'd 'ave 'oped you'd 'a known me better. In these situations it's customary to say, 'Albert, I'm in it. It was over my knees some days ago, it reached my waist at the weekend, and I'm now threatening to sink beneath it altogether.' If you were short of time, yer could just say, 'Albert, I'm in the shit. 'Elp!' Either way, I'd know what I'm dealing with, and you'd get me up there pronto."

Hmm, typical. "Alright, Albert, I need help, please."

"Thank you. That wasn't so bad, was it, boss? Now, what can I do to 'elp yer, and where do you need me?"

EIGHTEEN

The Right Lines?

A S WE'D ARRANGED after the carol service, Alex was to meet me at my London club, where we would be joined by Albert for lunch. The purpose was to introduce Albert to Alex, and to persuade Alex to have a few shooting lessons from the world champion, just to polish his technique up. In addition, I anticipated Albert would be a bulwark against tricks from the belted earl... perish the thought!

The Athenaeum, grand but faded, was originally the haunt of bishops and intellectuals, but by the mid eighties it had fallen on slightly hard times. Of necessity it had become rather more catholic in its admission policies, and that's when I joined. Without question it was an enjoyable place to lunch, and a wholly suitable place to meet with Alex. Its suitability as a venue for Albert, with his rather more extrovert style, remained to be seen.

I had briefed Albert at length on the best way to tackle Alex: "Don't! Leave him to me"; the dress code to follow: "No tie, no admission", to which Albert had simply said, "If I must, boss"; and the need to respect the atmosphere of cloistered calm the club liked to cultivate. It was on this last point I was least comfortable; I was briefing the bull who was about to be given access to the china shop. However, although I recognised that Albert was very good at creating crises, under cover of the resulting chaos a resolution would often emerge. Nonetheless, I approached this meeting with trepidation. Albert was not the most likely of bedfellows for a scion of an original Norman conqueror, but hell, stranger things had happened. After all, as a boy from the valleys neither was I.

I turned off Pall Mall and into the club a little early. It had not been one of my better days; the stock market had just gone into free fall, slicing more than a third off my paper wealth. While the money tied up in my little bet was not huge, I could have done without being called on to find the £6,000 I was effectively underwriting. In addition I had just agreed to buy Pogle's Wood, the patch of woodland outside Pinch-Me-Near-Forest. The lady owner, having invested all her fortune into various crackpot business ventures with the League Against Cruel Sports, had ended up in the bankruptcy courts. As a result, the rather magical Pogle's Wood had come on to the market, and I was hoping to turn it into a nature reserve, which would be a first in this part of Blankshire. I enjoyed wandering in Pogle's Wood during the summer, and I knew that if I didn't complete on the promise to buy it quickly some jobbing builders, whose intentions were less community focused, were also after it. The fact it was rumoured to be well foxed for the Blankshire was, of course, incidental. The only trouble was, buying Pogle's Wood *and* bailing out the Blankshire if Alex failed to outshoot the belted earl was going to give me the sort of sleepless nights I thought I'd said goodbye to when I sold my firm. Therefore, my mood was not of the best. However, smile and the world smiles with you.

So I sauntered into the club, apparently a man without a care. Alex, to his credit, was on time, every inch the perfectly attired country gent come to town.

"Afternoon, Alex, good to see you."

"Afternoon, Hector. Bit scruffy, this old place. Not been here since an aged bishop uncle of mine retired. He practically lived in the place, but that was twenty years ago."

"Alex, I know today has been a bit of a mystery, but it does actually have a purpose, apart from the very good lunch I promised you. Now, thing is, I was talking to the belted earl a couple of weeks ago. As you know, when Philip Q approached him about the auction just before Christmas, he sent Philip away with a super sized flea plus eggs in his ear. Not a nice experience for him, by all accounts. Well, the earl and I got to talking, as you do…"

"Not with that fella, I don't," growled Alex.

"Anyway, we got to talking about your shooting day on the fifteenth. You know, when he visits you."

Alex just had to interrupt. "One tradition I've never managed to shake off. Family's been doing it for years, and in fairness to the fella, he does a decent day back at his place to finish the season."

Ignoring the interruption, I continued regardless. "We talked about the joint enterprise, the auction. Needless to say, he'd made his views abundantly plain to Phil Q-H, so I didn't even bother asking. Instead I tried another tack. I decided, off my own bat and at my cost, that perhaps a little wager between consenting adults might be in order, and he was quite receptive to the idea. I'd say he's a bit of a bandit on the quiet."

Curious now despite himself, Alex was attentive. "A wager eh? Well I'm told he can be a bit of a one for that stuff, not that I'd ever listen to gossip, but I know he likes the odds being right. Quite crafty he is. The stories one hears are not flattering. Trust you have a long spoon, supping with the devil and all that. Look, Hector, it's your business, but if he was receptive I think you'll find it means he knows something you don't. Murky waters often swirl around that fella, so I hear, and I'd be worried for you, what?"

As always, Alex knew far more about his rival than he was admitting to.

"Alex, I think we have the earl buster on hand. You'll meet him in a minute. In the meantime tell me, of the two of you, how do you rate the earl as a shot?"

"Well, the fella is pretty renowned for his marksmanship, I have to admit. On a good day I might give him a run, but to be honest, he does get an awful lot of practice. Nothing else to do, yer see, so as a non gambling man I'd be putting my money on him."

"Yes, I thought you'd say that. Well you'll be interested to hear that he has agreed to donate a day and £2,000 extra, say £6,000 in all, to the auction, and I don't want to worry you but it's all down to you. As long as you can even the score with him on your shooting day he will honour this promise, which means we get everyone else on side too. Now, the chap we are about to meet, my friend Albert, is going to help us keep the odds fair. Thing is, I agree with you. We can practically guarantee there will be some funny business from the earl one way or another, and I reckon if we can spot it early and rumble him, it will blow his confidence.

"Still think it'll be tricky. Like trying to catch a greased seal, slippery isn't the half of it with that man."

"I know what you mean, but fighting fire with fire is what I think is needed. To help you outshoot him you're going to have to listen to someone. I know you've been shooting since people were using flintlocks, but Albert without question will add a little extra refinement to any man's shooting. He's bloody good, believe me, and very astute, so please, please, please be a little patient. When he arrives let me do the talking, and when you're happy and relaxed, listen to what he has to say. Enjoy getting the free advice of one of the best shots in the world, it'll make all the difference. Remember, it's my cash that's riding on you."

I had thought of illustrating my confidence by explaining the devious beauty of the Albert Hop, but decided against it. Alex's hearing wasn't what it had been – had it declined because he had long ago ceased to listen, or had he ceased to listen because of his hearing? It was a moot point. Either way, the Albert Hop would have been an explanation too far. Alex was far from being convinced, but he was listening which was about as good as it would get.

"Well, Hector, I s'pose we can all learn. Agreed. 'Free' sounds pretty good, too." He grinned, a hint of nerves showing an underlying lack of confidence about tackling something new. I had to tread very warily now. Like a gazelle in the African bush, Alex could be easily startled and never be seen in these parts again. For now, however, he was being brave.

"Now, you getting involved to help us raise the money, obviously I'm all in favour of that, but these are deep waters you're fishing in. I'm willing to help, made that clear, but I'm not at all sure what the plan is. You've been a bit mysterious. I am a Bicester, and now I'm head of the family, so I do have my integrity to think of. Very important, that is."

I sighed. Him and his bloody integrity. No wonder nothing interesting had ever happened to him; so much which might have been good for him had failed the wretched integrity test – or rather, the 'What would the ancestors think?' test. As if they cared, wherever they might be!

"Look, Alex, it's pretty straightforward. Let's meet with my friend Albert, we can chat about the shooting day, and I'll see if he is willing to help. Don't forget, he has a very successful shoot in Norfolk, and if he agrees to help it will be as a favour to me. Have a little patience, and let's see what he comes up with. Think how much better off we, and the estate, will be if we can get this right."

A scowl of dissatisfaction from Alex. I think he was rapidly reaching his input threshold; never high, it would quickly be exhausted. Further evidence of cornered aristo syndrome appeared when Alex played his 'Get out of jail if unhappy with events' card.

"Well, don't forget I'm really here in London for a trustees meeting. Got to be there at three, and of course..."

Thump! I quivered and shot forward, nearly collapsing in the process. It could only be...yes. I turned round, shoulders ringing and stinging. "Albert, you old fool. What did you do that for?" "What, gov?" Albert asked, great beaming ruddy face a picture of happy contentment. The limelight was his. "Ain't yer pleased to see me? What's wrong with yer? Most people are delighted when I makes an appearance, not looking hurt and shook up. You all right? Nothing bad happened, has it? No horrible disease?"

I paused, working the muscles in my back gingerly. All sorts of protests sprang to mind, but there was no point. This was the point: Albert was making an entrance, and I had been reduced to the role of a prop. If I chose to play with fissile material...

"Albert, allow me to introduce you to the Hon Alexander, strictly Lord Blankshire, my fellow Joint Master and owner of some of the finest shooting in the whole of England."

"Well pleased and delighted, squire," Albert responded. "Well known to me your little gaff is. 'Eard a fair bit about it. Of course, being where you are, the topography around there, you'd be ashamed of yourself if it wasn't good shooting, wouldn't yer? Or, at least, you'd be changing head keepers."

Albert had thrown so much over familiarity and knowledge into one speech that I could see Alex's brain was reeling. He had "Does not compute" written all over his face. If I wasn't careful he'd be heading for the exit; too much novelty on first acquaintance would be daunting for him.

"Albert, Albert, slow down. Let me get you both a drink and we can start at the beginning."

"Alright, squire, whatever you say. In the meantime, just a quick un: is there a phone in this dump of yours? Just gotta to speak to a geezer. It'll only be a quick call, got some Ruskies to sort out."

"Albert, this place is not a dump!" Even I felt slightly indignant. We looked around at the ornate marble-pillared hall with its striking ceremonial curved staircase. Pity about the water damage staining the far wall, but dump it was not.

"You know me, 'Ector, I like things pristine. This wants knocking down and rebuilding." In Albert's relentless quest for his idea of perfection that probably would have been the simplest solution.

"Look, Albert, over there by the porter's lodge is the club phone. Tell the porter it's on my account." No doubt I would be picking up the bill for Albert's long distance shoutathon to the USSR. The mood he was in he could have raised his voice a bit outside and he would have been heard in Moscow. As Albert slid towards the old-fashioned wooden phone booth, Alex grabbed my arm.

"Who is that fellow? He's very noisy. Am I really going to have to spend the whole of luncheon with him?"

I had known the first ten minutes were going to be the most difficult to manage, and I was being proved right. I had tried to brief Albert, but the bull was in the china shop and his bovine spirits were in the ascendency. The need for Albert to use the phone was helpful as it meant I could guide Alex to the dining room, help him to a very large gin and tonic, and soothe a little of his caution with the warm embrace of alcohol. I would also try reason, although with rather less confidence.

"Fact is, if Albert can help us, he will guarantee another

£30K into the hunt. We'll fix the stables, and help fine-tune your shooting into the bargain."

"Well, I'm not sure I like the fella. Awfully forward, isn't he?"

"Alex, he's the same with everyone. He's won his clay shooting championship seven times, and he has an Olympic medal, so he's pretty good, you know."

"Not sure Charlotte would approve." This was said in the tone of a small boy who has run out of excuses not to go to bed at the agreed hour, and was reduced to saying "wont!"

"Alex, since when have you ever let that worry you? Charlotte's not here, is she?" Hmm, I realised my tone was not helpful. I was going to create resentment if I wasn't careful, and that might turn to stubbornness quicker than London snow can turn to slush. Alex was clearly not minded to be overly helpful – could Albert and I pull a rabbit out of the bag?

NINETEEN

Chuff Chuff

ALBERT STRODE ACROSS the dining hall, cuffs halfway up his lower arms and tie already slightly askew, swaying artfully around tables with a grace that belied his size. The likelihood of him making it through lunch without his top button popping open was remote. Albert grinned cheerfully, the very soul of a contented man, while Alex grimaced at me. Really, at times he could be Lord Dismal of Desmond Hall.

Albert collapsed himself on to the vacant chair between us and grabbed the conversation by the scruff of the neck. "Now then, Al. You don't mind if I call you Al, do you?" This was said with a grin I recognised. It was the "Leave it to me, Guv" look I'd last seen shortly before the Albert Hop was unveiled on an unsuspecting world.

"Well..." Alex hesitated. "Most people call me Alex, but anyway..."

"So, Al, tell me about the shooting on your little place. Going well, is it?" Albert was attempting to burst through carefully constructed barriers of reserve that others had spent twenty years stalking around. I was riveted. However, when the fireworks did arrive later, they came from a direction no one could have predicted. The lunch settled into a sort of a pattern which was clearly not comfy for Alex. If Albert was aware of the diffidence and colossal lack of engagement, he did a good job of ignoring it. In Alex he had, in fairness, a genuinely knowledgeable listener, one who knew his stuff when it came to shooting. At no point, however, did enthusiasm threaten to intrude. A bottle of decent red was consumed, but between three of us it was a lunch notable for sobriety.

As is so often with these occasions, the real point of the matter was scrupulously ignored until we got to the pudding. Or, at least, it would have been if fate had not intervened. I had just started setting the scene.

"For the day in question, we will be down by the old railway line…"

"Ah." A sharp intake of breath from Albert as he picked up the conversation. "That'll be interesting. See, I'm fascinated by old railway lines. You're talking about the Malsham Swerver?"

"Sorry Albert? The Malsham Swerver, did you say? I'm not sure…"

Alex interrupted, for the first time a faint gleam of real interest in his eyes. "Yes, of course he is. Hector, I'd have thought you'd know that. It's called The Swerver because the railway line was built around various hills, as it navigates between Malsham and Little Todlingon, that was where the depot was you know. Far end of Little Toddlingon actually, do you know it?" I suspect my expression spoke volumes. Alex resumed, now addressing his remarks to the apparently rapt Albert. So, as I was saying, it swerves in and out of the Blankshire wolds, you see? Been gone thirty years now. When I used to sleep in the attic of the Big House during the war, one of my happier memories is of listening to the goods trains. Always moving limestone from the local quarries. We could hear the echo of the steam whistle in the night air. Do you know, I used to reckon I could tell the individual locos by the noise they made, especially the little Saddleback shunters. Now that was a shunter to get excited about..."

He hesitated, summoned his courage, and for the first time addressed a question to Albert.

"Albert, tell me, how on earth do you know about our forgotten little railway line, winding its way across my land?"

"Well you see, Al, and this is not a secret I share wiv many people, I'm a bit of an expert on old trains. Fascinated by them, I am. I checked out for old lines around you before accepting this, hmm...yer know, particular assignment." Albert glanced around as we digested this confession, then went on. "Chairman of the Norwich to Melton Constable Railway Trust, I am. Well actually, I own it. Always been a great interest of mine. We, that is me mainly, want to restore the old line properly. It runs through my shoot, but hell, it's the sound of those trains, especially the Saddleback shunters. I'm restoring one of them myself, yer know. From 1903 it is. Yup, spent years at it, we 'ave, and nearly finished now we are. What do you think of that? Ain't it something?"

He beamed, safe in the knowledge that this was possibly the pinnacle of human achievement, and now Alex was all ears.

"What, you're restoring a Saddleback? Now that does get the old grey cells going, you lucky chap."

"Well yes, that's what I said," Albert breezed. "Bloody good fun it's been, too. Secured the engine parts for a song. Marvellous thing it will be too when it's completely finished. Just imagine it, chief..."

Quiet descended. Both Alex and Albert went slightly misty eyed as they contemplated the potential marvels of a fully restored Saddleback. After an appropriate pause to savour the metaphysical pleasure of this idea, Albert proceeded to enlighten us about his ambitious plans to revive the wretched railway line he now owned. This took some time, and I was happy to allow all the information to enter one ear and exit the other with no chance of it troubling either my memory cells or cognitive functions. In short, I hadn't the faintest idea or interest in what they were now talking about.

Alex was the first to return to the here and now. Gulping a great mouthful of wine, he started talking in newly confident but confidential tone.

"Well, it's a funny thing. I'd love to find a way to bring at least a part of the abandoned Swerver line back to life, perhaps run a Saddleback into the old quarry, have some points and a couple of sidings, just like the old days. Can you imagine the fun we might have, playing proper trains? We can get Old Preston, the retired head keeper, to help us. He's a good chap. See, the thing is, I've got the frame of an old Saddleback discreetly tucked away in a barn on the far side of the estate. Bit of a secret, if you must know. I don't share everything with Charlotte."

A furtive look flickered across Alex's face. Albert ignored it, grabbed him by the arm, and looked at him fondly. "Never thought a fella like you would be a man after my own heart, not after the build up 'im over there gave you…" Albert nodded in my direction. "Old misery, indeed. Quite a turn up, I'd say this is. Pleasure to meet you, boss."

All thoughts about the day's shooting and our need to outwit the belted earl had now clearly fled. These two wanted only to talk about trains. Alex, ignoring me completely, leaned over earnestly.

"The thing is, Albert – I may call you Albert, mayn't I? It's one my greatest dreams to get some of the line back in working order so that once again the night air will echo with the sound of the Saddleback locos, what?" He paused, looked around, and, with a silly grin, added, "What do you think of this?" Then he cupped his hands, took a great mouthful of air, and made the most abominable drawn out whistling noise.

"Oops, sorry. Bit loud that, but you know what I mean?" he asked, looking to his new best friend for approbation. Well might he look to Albert, he wasn't going to get it from me.

The sounds of fellow club members eating slowed appreciably in the background.

"What?" said Albert. "You reckon that sounds like a Saddleback? Nah, I don't think so, chief. Now, this sounds like a Saddleback." He put his hands to his lips and produced an ear splitting whistle that was, if anything, more piercing than the one produced by Alex. If only – but of course, it was too late. The memo to Alex, that should have been written before this lunch, would have said, "DO NOT GET IN A PISSING COMPETION WITH ALBERT. HE ALWAYS WINS!"

I was hypnotised by the spectacle unfolding, or was it building up a head of steam, in front of my eyes, and I was not the only one. The club restaurant was reduced to near silence, knives and forks hovering in mid air, nervous glances shooting in our direction from all corners. The Athenaeum liked to think of itself as cloistered – sepulchral was often nearer the mark – but not today. Not with my train enthusiast friends burbling, chuffing, and whistling away.

Alex suddenly became aware that perhaps his excess of unaccustomed enthusiasm was not wholly appreciated. Grabbing Albert, who was merely getting warmed up, by the arm, he said, "I say, old chap, let's be a little discreet. I think they are not quite as keen on these things as you and me."

"Fair point, guv, but you did start it," observed Albert, companionably and accurately.

"Well anyway, there's something I could really do with knowing. Now look, Albert..." Clearly Alex wanted something, which was most unlike him. In my experience he had never asked another human being for a favour, and I felt this new found matiness had gone quite far enough. Hoping to return to the original point of the luncheon, I stood to interrupt.

"Look, Alex, we have twenty minutes before your important trustees meeting starts. Don't you think we ought to be…" I might as well have stood in front of a runaway steamroller.

Alex hesitated, thought quietly for a moment, then, "Balls to it! Do you know how many hours I've spent in those damned meetings? Tax lawyers, accountants, QCs, land agents. All think they are twice as clever as me, telling me my bloody business. We never accomplish much, sometimes agreeing the date for the next meeting is as good as it gets. And spending the estate's money, of course. Well, just for once they can wait. After all, they can't start without me, and this, now this is important."

The unaccustomed light of rebellion burnt bright. He returned his attention to Albert, a look of quiet pleading in his eyes. "Albert, as one enthusiast to another, can you tell me how I get the parts to rebuild a Saddleback?"

Albert sucked his breath in through pursed lips, every inch the hard-pressed British worker about to impart bad news. "Ah well, you see, Al, bit of a state secret, that is. Not one I really share, not generally anyway." Pause. "Gotta protect your sources, is what I've learnt, anyhows." Albert had a conspiratorial look now. "It's not what you know, its 'oo, if you get my meaning. But, seeing as how you and I are going to be working together, in a manner of speaking" for the first time in a while, Albert acknowledged my presence with a wink "a fella 'oo shoots with us at my place in Norfolk, found out he has connections with the old yards at Barry Docks. You know, in South Wales where all the old locos went to be cut up. Well I discovered he knows a geezer 'oo knows a man 'oo 'as supplies. Best ask no questions,

153

I always says. Anyway, rumour is this guy worked there for tweny years, and walked out every day with a different part under his jacket. Can yer believe it? Anyway, wot is beyond question is 'e now 'as a pretty decent supply of the necessary parts. Very hush-hush now."

"Yes, yes, of course," said Alex, the famous integrity forgotten. "So, you can help with the parts then?" This was said in the tone of a penniless alcoholic being offered a drink by a new found friend, a hint of desperation under the studied casualness. Albert beamed at him, as always revelling in the spotlight as he gained another acolyte.

"Well, chief, I reckon, I just reckon, maybe." He paused. "We might be able to do something. What you need to do now is tell me exactly what you've got stashed away in that shed of yours, and then I can talk to my, ahem, friend, and see what can be done. Not without optimism, I'm not." Albert enjoyed under promising. I took this as meaning the job was as good as done, and Alex looked encouraged.

"I have a long list, you know. Everything itemised that will be needed to restore her to perfect running order. Old Preston and I have spent most of the winter working on the original plans, trying to establish what is needed. It's been a labour of love, I can tell you."

"Her", indeed! I could sense the conversation was heading towards an itemised listing of parts necessary to get a 1903 Saddleback chuff chuff steaming again. Purgatory for the non-committed.

"Should we go and grab a quick coffee upstairs in the library?" I asked. This broke the lovers' clinch, if only temporarily. Albert headed for the gents, and suddenly Alex was at my arm.

"You know what, he's not a bad fellow, that Albert. Obviously he's not really like me, but he knows an awful lot about shooting, and, better than that, he can help me with my plan to get the Saddleback trains running out to the quarry again. Been dreaming of finding someone of his calibre for years. Was told such fellers didn't really exist any more, or you had to pay through the nose for them. Shows what happens when I listen to my clerk of the works." Only Alex would still have a Clerk of the Works.

At that point my long time business associate Dave, responsible for my original introduction to the Athenaeum, waved at me. I had often thought of having a slogan T-shirt made especially for him, saying, "Club bore, just add wine", and never was it more true than this afternoon. He had clearly lunched well but non too wisely and was florid of complexion, looking every day of his fifty-four years.

"Hector! Hector! Come over, we need to catch up."

Alex sidled away from my tender care to get himself some coffee. It took me twenty minutes to escape from Dave, and I was becoming increasingly aware as he chatted of whoop whoops coming from the library, punctuated by the occasional shrill whistle. I realised that the planning of the new track beds for the Malsham Swerver quarry branch line was threatening to get out of hand. Making a conscious effort I finally disentangled myself from Dave and headed for the library.

I hoped my guests would be drinking coffee and nothing stronger. If Alex turned up to his trustees meeting a good hour late and full of something stronger than the joys of steam power I would truly have Charlotte on my case, but it turned out that talk of steam was the only intoxicant the two of them needed. Seated with a large club table between them, they had two dozen or so coffee spoons arrayed in neat lines and rows to denote the various tracks within the planned quarry sidings. The talk was lively.

"Thing is, Al, from what I can remember from the map there was a bridge into the quarry. Is it still there?"

"But of course, old boy. Think I'd let 'em knock that down? That's the way we'll get the track bed in, then the track, and then the Saddleback." Alex grinned, clearly proud of his foresight, and Albert was being effusive.

"Well, Al, I reckon you've thought of a lot. Do you think you'll run to a new engine shed too?"

"Well, obviously! That's exactly what I'm planning, what do you take me for?" The answer "An idiot" rose in my breast, but I swallowed my words. The conversation moved on, rapid-fire. Blink and, if you were lucky, you would have missed it. I wished I had.

Albert and Alex were demonstrating to one another the respective merits in terms of sound of the old-fashioned single cylinder boiler versus the more modern compound cylinder. After listening to them for five minutes, I was considerably better informed but none the wiser, and the vocal demonstration meant every club member within earshot was watching these two idiots. They shuffled coffee cups around their imaginary sidings, making the appropriate sounds, which were all different depending on the signals and the direction of travel. I realised this was the little symphony of discords I had been hearing from the hall, and Alex was enthusiastically leading the charge.

"No one really appreciates now how beautiful these old single cylinders sound." Here he gave out the appropriate cry. "They were just right, you know, which was why they were still in use after forty years."

Any second now my club membership would be in jeopardy. As if on cue, the library steward approached me. Briefly my two friends paused to see how I would deal with the intrusion.

"Are these two your guests, sir?"

I rose to deal with this out of the earshot of my guests. "Well, yes they are, actually. The chap on the left is Lord

Blankshire, and opposite him is my friend Albert, world clay pigeon shooting champion."

"That's as maybe, sir, but one or two of the club members are unhappy at the noise."

There was something about his manner. "Have any other members actually complained yet?" I asked. "Not yet, sir, but we do like everyone to enjoy the hushed ambience appropriate to a library."

"When you say ambience, I take it you mean silence. Don't you think we'll all have enough of that in the grave? These two are simply having a lively and informed debate on a major project of industrial archeology. Just the sort of thing the club was founded to promote, rather than having us all sitting around like stuffed dummies."

"Well...sir...I, ummm," he stuttered.

"I shall make a suggestion. If someone complains, I will ask my good and esteemed friends to tone things down. In the meantime, everyone seems to be rather enjoying the display." While not personally over impressed by the turn of events, I was not going to allow the nascent friendship to be unnecessarily interrupted. I glanced behind me. Alex was quiet and had assumed a beatific expression. He was clearly miles away, dreaming of a glorious spring day, blue bells ablueing and primroses abloom, when he would finally ascend the footplate of his newly refurbished Saddleback. Lovingly polished, with muted blacks and freshly gleamed brass work, the loco would be fired up by the ever loyal Old Preston, ready for the instruction.

"Signal at green. Ready to proceed, sir?"

"Steam ahead then, Preston old boy." And then, setting hearts aswelling, the great iron monster would lurch forward...

Silly old fool, but there was no accounting for folks. Not even ones as posh as Alex. He snapped out of his reverie as

I wandered over and sought to bring the original purpose of our lunch to a conclusion.

"Look, chaps, are you two content here? I was just wondering if we could spare five minutes to talk about the shoot off."

"No need," said Alex.

"Quite right, squire," piped up Albert. "We've discussed it."

"We have a plan. Not complicated."

"Quite remarkably straightforward."

"We," said Alex, "have talked this little problem through. Considered various options when you were talking to that red faced chap, and now we're agreed. As my friend said, we have a plan, no need to trouble you with it. Quite sufficient if Albert and I are behind it, and, of course, Albert will be staying with me at the Rectory. Lots to discuss, eh Albert?"

"Sure, is boss. Nothing we can't handle with a good recce, though."

"We reckon it's foolproof."

I decided this insane billing, cooing, and chuffing had gone on for long enough.

"Gentleman, perhaps we can adjourn." Alex, now his next date with Albert had been fixed up, seemed inclined to recover his reason.

"Sorry, Albert, duty calls, but we can pick this up again. Perhaps you'd better get to me a day or two early. There'll be a lot to talk about, railway matters as well as our foolproof plan to win the shoot off."

Foolproof indeed! They had not reckoned with the nefarious ways of the belted earl.

TWENTY

Brekko

I CALLED ALBERT a couple of days after our steaming lunch. "So, Albert, what did you think of the old boy?"

"Well, 'ave to say, I like 'im. In fact, I won't 'ear a word against 'im. Guess wot? Up to Blankshire on the thirteenth, I am. Dinner party that night at 'is house, going to have a look at his ol' Saddleback. Got to do that, and recce of the quarry, examination of the sidings naturally, then check out the old railway bridge. Yer know, the one into the quarry, which he tells me will still be up to weight."

As Albert paused to catch his breath I felt mounting irritation.

"What, your weight or the train's?" I snapped.

So far, all I'd heard was that Albert's proposed jaunt involved an awful lot of self indulgent train spotting and nothing to ensure that a plan was in a place to help Alex defeat the belted earl and save my money.

Albert sounded mildly offended, but not defensive. "Now, now, you're not, if I may venture, being as kind as you might be, especially given the time and consideration I have given this matter of yours. And my time is valuable to me. Don't forget that, my friend. One of us still 'as to earn a living, and it ain't you, that's for sure."

Here Albert slowed his words, lost most of his distinctive

demotic style and enunciated with precision. I was to sit at the feet of the master and be taught.

"What you have to remember, you see, is that shooting involves emptying the mind of all extraneous matter. My new friend needs to attain a state of Zen-like tranquility, his mind devoid of all thought, so there is nothing to interfere between the eye and the trigger finger. Now, I can see you thinking that, in the empty mind stakes, my new friend, the Hon Alexander, Lord Blankshire himself, has a clear head start over us lesser mortals. But that, please, is unfair. Shooting requires confidence, not intellect, so it is a vital part of my mission to ensure he is buoyant, full of the joys of his own wonderfulness. As you might well have noticed, it seems to work for me!"

I imagined him beaming at me in that faux foolish way of his that I knew so well, as the lecture in sporting psychology continued.

"We 'ave to remember that he's spent most of 'is life being bested, and on occasions monstered, by the belted earl. Therefore, his natural levels of confidence will not be of the highest order. If I can get him thinking and talking about 'is railway line, 'e won't be thinking and worrying about his shooting. Stands to reason! So you be a little kinder, if you don't mind, about my little railway odyssey. It's not quite the diversion you might think. Yes, we are going to sneak away and do a little feasibility study of reviving the thing, and yes, we will 'ave a proper look at the Saddleback shunter itself. 'E's very keen, yer know. Sent me the pictures and everything, marked private and confidential. Not bad, neither, they ain't. I've been doing some research..."

"Albert, Albert, please! Look, I know you're gripped by that wretched train, but I'm afraid I don't share your interest. What I want to know is: what's the PLAN?"

"Well, beyond one or two little trade secrets, which

160

I share with no man, truth of the matter is I dunno. We just have to be a little flexible. Me and the ole boy 'ave done a fair bit of planning work already. 'E's not a bad little shot when 'is mind is kept right, I reckon. So it's simple. The way I sees it, I get 'im feeling on top of the world, give 'im a bit of shooting practice, then worry about what stunts 'is deadly rival might pull. Finally, I might just 'ave a rabbit or two in the bag myself. Remember your phrase, 'fighting fire with fire'? Well, believe me, I can do that. But if 'is Lordy Earlship plays fair, we will too. Anyway, for now what I'm gonna do is accept the kind invitation to revel and wallow in railway nostalgia. Then I'll walk the course, so to speak, talk to 'is beaters, and generally get a sense of what might be possible."

I sighed. Clearly the infection of love for the proposed railway line had bitten deep. To my mind, Albert was wallowing far too deeply in the railway matters, but this suggestion did not go down well.

"Look, my son, you have to admit I've had Alex surfing on a wave of ebulliance. 'Oo would of thought that was possible? Just remember what faith moves. I suggest you leave me to it, we'll sort the bad old h'earl out, never you fear. Now, I'm off. Urgent research to do, if you know what I mean."

Even at 200 miles, I could feel the knowing wink that Albert used in tricky situations beaming down the phone to me. In a mood of resignation I hung up. It was not so much the money, loath though I was to spend my money burnishing the earl's lofty social position, it was that I just didn't want the old devil to win.

Anyway, for now the matter was out of my hands. I watched the long range forecast carefully, and it would seem the special day would have good weather for shooting. I went off and had a few hours shooting practice myself, although my competence was unlikely to have much, if any, effect on the outcome of the duel itself. Given the quality of my shooting, this was probably a good thing. As other events filled my life and we had a few decent days hunting, I realised I had to trust Albert.

Talking to a gamekeeper one day I heard a suggestion that someone was looking to buy up owls – yes, owls – on an industrial scale. I quizzed the man, but he was vague. It was just a rumour he'd heard that if anyone had inadvertently trapped an owl there might be a bit of a market for it. I filed this information away under odd but irrelevant.

Time passed with no communications from my rotund friend. The thirteenth came round, and I guessed he had arrived in Blankshire and was engaged on train building activities with Alex.

Finally the day of the shoot itself rolled around. There had been no big pre-shoot blow out dinner, as this was essentially a domestic occasion. It was my duty to get to Alex's Big House for 8am prompt, so my gun, 400 cartridges, and I duly presented ourselves at the front door at the allotted time. Who should I see as I was guided into the very grand reception room but dear old Albert. Firmly ensconced on a huge antique sofa before a blazing fire, his bestockinged feet on a Chippendale foot stool, he looked every inch the proud tenant in possession for life in his tweed breeches and check shirt.

As soon as he saw me, he rocked to his feet and danced towards me in ebullient form. With a great bear hug and a grin, he said, "Ah, 'Ector my friend, the train! The train! Simply magnificent, it is. What fun I can have here."

"Albert, please tell me you have a plan for today."

"Today, what? Oh, yes. Yeah, of course. It'll be fine, I think. I'm getting on like a house on fire with the head keeper, Mr Preston, or Hey Presto, as I calls 'im. Sound chap. 'Es 'eard as I do a little sideline in albino pheasants. Yer didn't know that, did you? Little speciality of mine, they are. I've already supplied 'im with three dozen. Pleased as punch with 'em, 'e is. 'E reckons they'll add to the challenge. Thinks I agrees with him, but let's move on quickly..."

How we were to move on was not vouchsafed to me. Of course I had supreme confidence in Albert's ability, but this vagueness did concern me. Before I could pursue the question Alex ambled into the room, clutching various tatty looking documents. He glanced at me and waved vaguely in welcome, then focused on his new best friend.

"Albert, I say, you really must see these. I've been checking the old family archives, and found a wealth of old material from around the time of the building of the railway line. Amazed I never thought to look this stuff out before."

As ever, Alex was proceeding down a branch line of his own choosing, which seemed to have little connection with the main line events of the day. Albert, clearly recognising the difference between an empty mind and one full of irrelevance, took steps to get Alex back on the right tracks.

"Al! Look, Al, I think we ought to get up steam and get on wiv breakfast. Wouldn't do to keep the guests waiting, would it? I think I can 'ear the sound of 'em arrivin'." The candlestick maker's boy from Norwich giving one of Britain's premier barons lessons on etiquette was a sight I found the patience to savour. Alex sighed wearily.

"Yes, yes, I suppose you're quite right. If we must, let's go and meet the earl et al."

The doorbell clanged in the background, punctuated by the incongruous sound of a novelty electrical doorbell. I gathered this was one of the Dowager Lady Susan's ideas, and so the tones of "Delilah" rang out in a discordant melee of noise. The various guests swept in, ready for the day. They included the belted earl and his eldest son; Lettice, looking glamorously masculine in some very smart fitted tweeds and newly bobbed hair; William in a coat that was more hole than tweed and Perks, the land agent for the estate.

Lettice and I exchanged a kiss, and she led me by the hand through to breakfast. She liked and appreciated her friends did Lettice, and it appeared I had been promoted. The wager itself was a secret known to very few; the rest had no hint of the tension.

Breakfast passed agreeably, but rather without any great degree of good old-fashioned fun. Banter was notable mainly by its absence. It was only the presence of Lettice, chattering gaily to me, that made the thing bearable. Albert, by his extrovert standards, was taciturn, gazing into the middle distance, apparently lost in thought. Then, suddenly he was off.

As he passed me, he squeezed my shoulder. "Gonna check a few things out, boss."

I tucked into a mountainous plate of crispy bacon with all the necessaries, reminding me that breakfast was the one meal the English really excelled at. The belted earl conspicuously drew up a chair next to Alex and started chatting. Although a little too far away to hear clearly, I had a suspicion his chatter would involve a long series of niggles, with a good bit of finely honed gloating thrown in for good measure. The snatches of conversation that floated towards me tended to confirm my suspicion.

"Did you realise such and such?...Not looking good... Tatty, I'd say...Needs doing, I'd get on with it if I were you, eh, what?"

It was all stuff calculated to upset my friend, unused as he was to criticism of anything he chose to do on his little fiefdom. Its accuracy would only add to the irritation, and would also remind Alex that the belted earl ran his place to a standard of excellence unmatched in the whole of Blankshire.

As breakfast drew to an end, Alex looked pleased to be relieved of the belted earl's company. As I got up he joined me, and we wandered off together. As usual with this intensely shy man, I initiated the conversation.

"Albert tells me you're having a bit of fun with the old quarry."

Alex glanced at me nervously. "Has he told you about that?"

"Yes."

"Well, please be careful," this in a conspiratorial tone. "I've sort of mentioned it to Charlotte in passing, but I don't think she has quite detected the sniff of old locos or steam yet. At least there's been no hue and cry so far. Albert and I are doing a presentation at next month's estate board meeting. We had a little thinking tank, yer know, like they do in industry. Brainstorming, Albert called it, and we've prepared projections, coloured charts, a flow of cash thingie, and so on. It all looks pretty impressive to me. Light years ahead of the old ledgers we're using in the estate office, anyway. I don't see it's that unreasonable if we look to get a bit of cash back by reconstructing part of the estate's industrial history. I'll get everyone onside with the tourist potential. Longleat has lions, Alton Towers has things that whizz and induce vomiting, we'll have Saddlebacks. I'm learning all sorts of stuff from Albert. The man's a positive treasure."

Alex was as enthusiastic now as I'd ever seen him about anything. The usual nervous fidget had gone, and was replaced by a seldom seen look of steely determination. If he had been a washing powder, he would come with the caption: "New formula. Added backbone for maximum strength!" Whatever Albert had said had clearly produced the right galvanising effect. My cheque book lay a little easier in my pocket.

We walked out to the specially adopted if rather tatty

Land Rover, known as the gun bus, the belted earl striding in front. He didn't quite swagger, that was for lesser mortals and well beneath his dignity, but the clear impression was that he was on his toes. Having conducted some serious menacing of his rival over breakfast, he could go about his lawful business and let others think on.

The earl marched straight up to me, a hard, intense stare from his little boiled-sweet eyes belying the smiling countenance, gave me a quick, harsh handshake, and whispered, "Win or lose, all stays between us, eh? What?"

I was pretty sure that this was a one way sort of assurance. His defeat would be buried, but victory would be subtly circulated. Naturally, however, I gave my assurance. The two combatants had both done their preparation; battle was almost ready to commence.

TWENTY-ONE

Tranqs

B EFORE WE COULD move on to the first drive we had a routine piece of theatre to act out.

The thing about a shooting day, as with almost any sport, is that there is an element of luck. A footballer wants to play with the wind at his back, and a shooting man wants the bit of the line likely to produce the most birds. Typically, but not necessarily, this is the middle of the line. To try and ensure a stab at fairness each gun chooses a playing card from a pack of eight cards, and this determines his place in the line of guns. Although a little random, the right draw can make a day or ruin it, so to keep an element of fairness everyone shifts up a couple of places in the next line after each drive. Hence no one is stuck with an outside peg throughout the day.

The eight of us stood round: two noble scions of aristocracy, an heir each at their shoulders, William and Lettice Alex's land agent Perks, a modest man with much to be modest about, and finally the outsider, Hector from the principality of daffodils. 'Now, that is rum. Look at you', I thought to myself.

By a coincidence, the protagonists of this little drama were, for the first drive, drawn at opposite ends of the line. This meant that our two duellists would be apart from one another for large part of the day, to the obvious relief of

Alex. However, I saw a smile play across the face of the belted earl; not a good sign. Not for my cash, anyway.

We climbed into the gun bus, and off we rattled. Crash, bang, rumble, down pothole-infested tracks, splashing through huge puddles, bouncing on the seats, uncomfortably aware the seat springs had long since given up the ghost, heads skimming the roof. Finally we ascended a low rise and drew to a halt, disgorging from the gun bus like maggots pouring from a jar.

We started our trek along the old railway line to our designated positions. I saw the belted earl chatting busily to his henchman, his head keeper. In turn, his henchman spoke into a walkie talkie, which struck me as slightly unusual and perhaps ominous. Suddenly Albert appeared on a quad bike, bouncing over the ruts, his not inconsiderable frame flying a remarkable distance from the seat as he crested the low rise at some speed.

"Alright, boss," he saluted me as he ground to a halt. "Reckon something's cooking, I just don't know what. Anyway, I'm on the case."

As I wandered down to my place in the line I saw young Preston, whose lustful behaviour had sparked this entire drama. Upon the recent retirement of his soon to be train driver father, Old Preston he had become head keeper. It wasn't only the Blankshire toffs who liked to keep things in the family. He greeted me and offered to show me to my spot. I knew that, after the discovery of his affair with the hunt stable girl, Cassie, there had been tales of marital disharmony, so I decided to broach the question.

"How is Mrs Preston?"

"Had you not heard, sir? She's gone."

"Oh? Gone? I'm sorry to hear that, Preston."

"Well, truth is we haven't really been getting on for quite a while. Thing is, sir, our nightly activities had become rather infrequent. I've always been quite keen, but, sir, every night at 9pm, that was it. I was out like a light. In fact I was getting really worried, even went to see the doctor down in Upper Malsham. Well, to cut a long and rather embarrassing story short, they did various tests." He bent towards me, practically whispering. "It turns out, sir, she'd been putting horse tranquillisers in me tea. No wonder I was knocked out. Doctor, 'e was all set to call the police. Malicious or malevolent damage, or something like that, 'e said it was. Nasty situation, I don't mind telling you. Anyway, I confronted her, like. It was proper difficult. She got tearful, said she was fed up with me demands. Too much jiggy jiggy, not right at her time of life. A women was entitled to rest her bones at night, and not have them rocked about by the likes of me. Well, she'd never said anything like that to me before, not until we had this scene.

"I'm telling you, sir, because I want you to realise what a difficult situation I was in. Felt bad when I heard people talking about me and Cass behind our backs when we started getting quite, umm, friendly." Here he beamed, torn between embarrassment and pride at his exploits. Fortunately, on this occasion embarrassment won out, and I was spared the details. "It seemed to be the perfect solution. Mrs P has moved out, only into the next village mind, and now we're getting on better than we have for years. We're still married, so she pops in every night and makes me dinner, as you'd expect."

I didn't expect this, but comment seemed unnecessary. Young Preston continued with his illuminating insights into the domestic arrangements of a Blankshire gamekeeper.

"With Cassie, I, eerrmm…" He searched for euphemisms. I suspected his account of his activities to his peers would have been rather less delicately couched. "We see each other when we are feeling…anyway, sir, I'm sure you know what I mean."

Overall it was now much easier to understand what had driven him to chase the forbidden fruit. "Look, Preston, thank you for filling me on all this stuff. Better you don't advertise too much of it, I'd have said, but overall things seem to be working out quite nicely. Your, uuhhuumm, friendship with Cassie seems to be developing outside of working hours, Mrs Preston is getting a good night's sleep, and now we finally stand a better than even chance of getting the stables sorted. I wouldn't worry too much, if I were you."

My reflections on Preston's somewhat singular domestic arrangements were interrupted by the blast of a small trumpet that signalled the first drive was beginning. We'd soon enough learn who was going to be the victor of the little duel. With a few more paces we arrived at my spot, and so I unslung my gun and prepared to be entertained.

TWENTY-TWO

Beer

I HAD ALEX to the left of me, and to my right his oldest son. Albert was standing immediately behind Alex with his quad bike a few yards away. As always the affair began quietly. A few pigeons floated away above us, high in the sky, not the quarry for today. I enjoyed the peace and the time for contemplation, my shotgun cradled in my arms. Alex was practicing his swing, as important in shooting as in golf, and I could imagine the little rhythm that many of us use going through his head: "On it, past it, shoot it." This little bit of doggerel was designed to remind us that it was necessary to shoot in front of a flying pheasant to be sure of hitting it. Most of us, with the possible exception of Albert, seldom allowed enough distance to compensate for this very basic law of physics.

We were standing on the bottom edge of the Blankshire escarpment and the wooded slope rose spectacularly in front of us, the railway line skirting its edge. Unlike on my day in Norfolk with the Deadweights, a decent number of birds appeared, and, even better, they appeared over us. This drive, known as Tunnel Bridge, was the perfect spot for the sport. The birds, that were encouraged to live in the woods opposite us, would fly away from the racket the beaters were creating behind them via the easiest route, which was right over our heads. They would fly high but in reasonably straight lines; rather like some of today's guns had in life, I reflected. Young Preston had moved down the line, which ensured he had a decent view of both his employer and the belted earl. He, along with his opposite number from the belted earl's estate, Geoff Liversedge, were the official counters and referees for the day. Their judgments were final, and both took their responsibilities very seriously. Their livelihoods depended on it.

The birds were coming thick and fast. Although at the end of the line of guns, Alex seemed to be getting a really good showing. Watching him briefly, I could see an untroubled smoothness in his action that was a pleasure to watch. Clearly the little bit of buffing up from Albert had added an extra polish to his style that was standing him in good stead.

There was a steady crack of firing all around, reverberating up and down the valley, a wash of sound. Everyone had something to do; the only question was: would it be enough for Alex? Albert was whispering to Alex, this was a good sign; if anyone could assist Alex it was this man. I was beginning to thrill to my own shooting. A couple of birds flew high above me; swinging through them, firing two shots, gun punching shoulder once, twice; both birds crumpling and falling in front of me, all in an instant of time. The coveted left and right. This was not turning out to be such a bad day, despite the high stakes and imminent threat to my plans for Pinch-Me-Near-Forest.

I glanced over at Albert who was watching along the line, clearly a little agitated about something. Suddenly he straddled his quad bike; with a cough the engine caught, and he disappeared in a splitter-splatter of mud. The roar of the engine faded away as I focused on the job in hand. Despite, or perhaps because of, the fact I had the honour of the Daffodil Principality and outsiders everywhere at stake, not to mention my six grand, this shoot was becoming really exhilarating.

The birds continued to fly well, evenly spaced, a perfect and proper job. Even I, by no means the world's most accomplished shot, was producing a reasonable tally for someone's pot. This was shooting at its best: difficult but not unattainable birds; the satisfaction of the hunter; the hand and eye working together in some sort of harmony. So much better than my sporting recollections from school, being the Aunt Sally in the playground goal – again.

There was a lull. The barrel of my gun was warm; we had been busy. Young Preston, as expected, was keeping a beady eye on his employer behind me. He had a small counter in his hand and he was industriously clicking away as his boss added to the bag. It was clear Alex was in the form of his life. As long as he had a gun in his hands the birds were falling steadily; if not quite a monsoon, certainly a downpour. He was a pleasure to watch. An economy of movement and sureness of touch spoke of a youth every bit as misspent as one wasted in snooker halls, except, of course, this early foundation was now standing him in good stead.

A fresh bouquet of birds appeared. Momentarily, the sky darkened as a veritable blizzard of pheasants appeared above us, then, like the finale of a firework display, the crescendo of shooting increased until PPPAAAARRPPP! The hooter blew and the drive was over.

My gun barrel was too hot to touch, so I put my gun down and busied myself picking up my empty cartridges. Alex, either quicker off the mark or, more likely, knowing someone else would perform this menial task for him, wandered over.

"Well I think that went all right. Reckon I've never shot better. That'll give the fella something to think about. Mind you, I don't know where Albert is. He turned to me and said, 'You keep shooting like that, Al me old mucker,' I do wish he wouldn't call me Al 'and you won't need me. I'm just off to check they are drawing equally.' Truthfully I'm not quite sure what he meant, then he vanished. Rum 'un, eh? Sure he's got the best intentions. Fellow's a veritable Cheshire cat with that big grin of his. I like him, though, and he's improved my shooting no end, what?"

We walked back towards the gun bus.

"Well, Preston, how did we get on?" asked Alex.

"Well, sir, I counted sixteen off the drive for you off thirty-six shots. That's pretty good for Tunnel Bridge. You, sir" he pointed at me "got nine definite. Does forty-four shots sound about right?" His bright blue eyes flashed with quiet humour. Technically he might be the hired hand, but he knew I was a bit of a hack at this game, did young Preston, and he not afraid, in his polite way, to let me know it. I pretended not to hear and moved on. I hadn't had quite the same opportunity as some of the others to waste my youth on this rarified and expensive pursuit, and inwardly felt quite happy.

We caught up with Geoff, the earl's keeper. "'Is Lordship's going it some, sir. Dunno how you get the birds to fly so well, young Preston. 'Es done twenty-two, 'e 'as, off that drive. Mind you, took 'im forty-eight shots cos they're tricky, but 'e did do the number, so 'e's six ahead already by my reckoning."

Alex and I were happy to trust the two keepers to count honestly, particularly as they were taking turn and turn about. Geoff, unlike his boss, was a byword for integrity.

"Well, Alex," I remarked, "I thought you started really well there. Looks as though the coaching from Albert has really got you swinging through the birds well – wish I could say the same. The fellow at the other end has done well, though."

Alex was not listening. His brain was clearly in

overdrive, his eyes screwed up; some sentient thought was clearly taking place at the cost of some effort.

"All a bit odd, yer know, twenty-two at Tunnel Bridge," he was muttering, more to himself than to me, "and at the Tunnel End too. That's not quite right. We've never had that number of birds there…hmm, I think I need to talk to Albert, and quickly."

As if on cue, the roar of the quad bike ascended in our ears. Tearing down the track, the grime and mud spattered figure of Albert appeared. His big grin was gone, a frown in its place. Grinding to a halt he directed his attention at Alex, speaking crisply and firmly.

"Quick, boss, I've rumbled 'im. I know what 'es up to. I need beer, and lots of it."

"Sorry, you need what?"

"Beer, boss, and lots of it. No time to explain, but I need at least sixty tins"

"Albert, I'm surprised at…"

"Not for me! What do you think I am? Look, believe me, it's urgent." Alex finally grasped that Albert was not talking about personal consumption needs and produced the requisite answer.

"Mrs Preston, she's doing the catering today. She will be down at the folly behind the Big House, and she'll have plenty. At least the amount you need, anyway. Tell her I sent you."

Albert hoiked his frame back over the middle of the quad bike, and once again the mud flew as the clutch bit. As he left, I turned to Alex.

"I really don't know what that was about. I'm sure it's just a minor difficulty, but I feel better knowing Albert is on the case, that's for sure."

A grunt came from Alex as we joined the other shooters and climbed onboard the gun bus to swap tales of birds hit, heights achieved, accuracy won, and various goofs along the way. William and Lettice were chatting excitedly, and the offspring seemed to be getting on well.

The belted earl was sitting alone, aloof, quiet, composed and uninvolved, no doubt preparing himself for the second of five drives that day. Time for a little bit of cage rattling, I thought.

"Gather you saw your fair share of the sport on that drive?"

"Think you can say that I made the most of the showing. Not bad – well, not bad for round here, anyway."

"Noticed Alex had a good ratio of shots to birds."

"That's as maybe, but I'm well and truly ahead on the measure we agreed."

Ungracious even in victory, I thought. Tunnel Bridge was rightly renowned, and a compliment or two would not have gone amiss. I suspected there would be a big room in his Big House where all the compliments that he might have paid sat, labelled and graded according to value, and hoarded against a rainy day a mighty long time acoming.

"Yes, interesting how well things went on your side. Alex's new man has gone to check out a few new things. You've not met Albert, have you?"

"Not yet, no. I've heard of him, of course. Preparations around here always seem to need checking up on; we don't need that sort of thing over at my place, no indeed. I like to make sure everything is just so before my guests arrive. I think my people know how I work."

He slipped into a complacent silence as the gun bus began its slow lurching progression through the mud and ruts to the next drive. As we got out, a hamper containing hot coffee and sausage rolls appeared, together with, for those who were so inclined, a champagne and sloe gin cocktail: an interesting drink for 10.30am. On a day like this, starvation was never a possibility. After our refreshment break, we ambled to our next pegs.

I walked, my gun encased and sloped over my shoulder. This time the walk to my peg was shorter, and Alex was again near me. As we walked down Albert reappeared like a homing pigeon, this time with NEWS.

"I'm afraid you're down sixty tins of beer, boss."

"I'm what?"

"Yeah, I've been out confounding knavish tricks," Albert continued, grim faced. "I knew there would be a stunt somewhere, just couldn't work out what it'd be. Anyway, you know that footpath you and I talked about the other day, the 'ardly ever used one that goes through the left hand side of the drive you've just finished? Well, there was only a coach-load of bloody ramblers suddenly decided to wander that way. Spontaneously? I think not. Noisy lot too, according to the beaters, came through just as the drive began. Caused a lot of extra disturbance on the left, and yer can imagine the rest. Extra bloomin' birds everywhere, but mostly to the left, so no wonder nobody's friend will 'ave done so well. 'Is shooting wasn't as sharp as yours though, I hear, just 'e 'ad more to go at. It's worked for 'im, got 'im a bit of a start, it has. Sorry 'bout that, boss.

"Anyway, realising what was going on, I collected the beer and I collared the ramblers' leader. Shifty, weaselly fella, full of the right to roam nonsense, but had no thought for the right to get lead shot dropped on their 'eads from your guns going about their lawful business. Wouldn't discuss where they were off to next, and 'e 'ad a walkie talkie stickin' out of his pocket. Curious, that. All 'is mates looked pretty sheepish. Not sure many of 'em had done a lot o' ramblin' before. I reckon to the pub and back would have been about their limit.

"So I told 'em it was a tradition of the estate to never

interfere with anyone's right of way if we were shooting, but we would offer people a beer or two to compensate 'em for loss of amenity if they would keep clear, that sort 'o guff. Leader fella wasn't too pleased I can tell yer, but 'is mates clearly knew a deal when they saw it. Reckon, between us, someone 'ad slipped up and paid 'em in full before they began. Anyway, you've now got fifteen burly geezers sipping your lager over on the far side of the quarry steps. Don't reckon they'll bother us again…bloomin' sauce!"

Clearly the first attempt at sabotage had produced some success, and although it was now curtailed the belted earl was well ahead on points. All that was required was for him to sit on his advantage, shoot about as well as my friend, and the day would be his. An early blow had been struck, and I felt the anger beginning to grow.

Albert had his arms around Alex's shoulders, and the words "shunter" and "bridge" floated towards me. Clearly the preferred tactic was once again to clear Alex's mind of stress by imagining happy steam-filled days to come.

Albert came over to me, his eyes alive with thoughts that would not, in any light, be described as charitable. Like a wasps' nest that has been poked the contents were liable to come spilling out and fly in any direction, bent on revenge and the infliction of pain.

"Right, I've settled Alex as best I can. In fairness to the old boy, 'e's as cool as the proverbial cucumber. 'E thinks, with the way 'e's shooting, 'e still 'as the chance to get one up. You know, I agree with 'im. I'm off to 'ave a word with one or two people, see if we cannot even the scores a little."

TWENTY-THREE

Owls

As Albert roared off for the nth time that day, Alex and I resumed our positions. One of the inestimable advantages of being the owner of the shoot, and employer of all and sundry, is that the propensity of your employees to start without you is very limited. In fact, it doesn't happen.

Today proved no exception. We had come half a mile or so down the railway line and were actually opposite the famed quarry, future home of the wretched Saddleback. Human-free for the last thirty years, it was awash with perfect sites for the birds: thick undergrowth and towering trees, extending some way back from the railway line. The expectation was that, once the birds started flying from the gently sloping quarry banks and dense woodland, they would come fast and furiously. In all, we expected between us to shoot around 500 birds during the day. Young Preston reckoned that our duellists had, between them, accounted for thirty-eight on the first drive alone, and the rest of us had accounted for another sixty or so, leaving, in total, around 400 to go, and this drive promised to be the largest of the day. Albert resumed his position behind Alex, and I imagined the conversation would be a mixture of sweetness and cajoling, thoughts of future train games together with practical advice.

As the birds started to fly, occasional glances to my left showed that Alex and his shooting coach were becoming a pretty deadly combination. Again the drive produced the goods in the way that not only did young Preston proud, but also allowed Alex to really tuck in and show that, on this form, he was more than a match for the belted wizard at the far end.

Without the earlier unfortunate rambling intervention it was likely that Alex would have been in the lead, and by the time the hooter parped its doleful note he had clawed back a little of the earl's advantage. The latter was now only ahead by a total of four, and again Alex had, as measured by the shot to bird ratio, clearly been shooting better. The belted earl was chuntering about the inadequacies of those counting, as ever graceless in his advantage. He wasn't enjoying his lead, consumed instead by his fierce desire to win and anxiety to reign supreme. By comparison Alex, although behind, was clearly enjoying his day. For myself, the existing lead between two such equally matched adversaries loomed like a mountain, in my imagination at least.

The others climbed into the gun bus behind us and, shadowed by Albert's quad bike, we moved on towards the third and final drive along the railway line. We landed up beyond the quarry at a wood known as Fracture Wood, where at some stage the ground had slipped away to form an irregular dish. Heavily wooded now, it held the promise of some exciting sport. This time I was perched on the left of Alex and the belted earl due to the curiosities of the numbering system. Again the shooting during this drive was of the very best quality, but the early lead the belted earl had established was proving to be, as my dear mam would have said, a bit of a bugger.

At the end of the drive the belted earl's lead remained at four, but this was still decent. He'd shot fifty-seven birds over all three drive's to Alex's fifty-three, but curiously, and pleasingly, Alex was outwardly unphased by the pressure.

"Do yer know, I think I'm doing OK. I'd have settled for this before we started." Encouragingly, the pressure was beginning to mount on his rival. It had been at least twenty minutes since his last supercilious remark, unheard of from a man for whom this form of conversational gambit was his stock in trade. As the belted earl climbed on to the gun bus, just behind me and ahead of the others, he glanced at me, a trace of sweat on his brow.

"Well, Hector, you know who's still ahead? An offer for you, between ourselves of course: it's now fifty-seven plays fifty-three, so, tell you what, concede now and I might just chuck a grand into the fund. Good faith on my part, allow you to cut your losses…"

"Thomas, thanks for the offer, but…to be honest, I have plenty of faith already. It's good faith and it's in my friend Alex, so, as far as I'm concerned, the competition continues. The competition continues fairly, and without any stray rambling from you, if you know what I mean!" I winked at him. He flushed, but wisely kept his counsel.

While not yet a cornered rat, if he had possessed whiskers they would have been twitching furiously. Escape was definitely on the agenda; the thrill seeker had reached his limits. However, I was not about to allow him to beam himself up, or indeed use any other avenue of escape.

So after this, the final drive by the railway line, we moved on to the fourth drive of the day by Plantation Farm. Following that it would be the Old Mill to finish the day, then back to the Big House for a top drawer late lunch. For the losing duellist lunch threatened to be a deeply disagreeable and gloomy occasion: gloating pie followed by smug pudding would, without question, feature on the menu. Still, the evidence didn't encourage winning thoughts yet, but at least if we were going to go down it had been a decent fight.

The game went on. One formerly super self-confident defender of his misspent youth against a not dissimilarly skilled challenger. One intelligent, convinced of his own worth; the other unaware such possibilities existed.

Round four of the match was no less exciting than previous three drives. Both of our doughty peers were swinging their guns with intent, genuine and talented craftsmen at work. To watch these two was a pleasure, one that sportsmen the world over would appreciate. Grace and economy always make for good watching, but, alive and alert for little tricks, I still felt bruised by the efforts of the belted earl to spoil things on the first drive, or at least rig the deck in his favour.

Fate was now not being kind to Alex. Although standing, by the logic of the draw, quite close to the earl, the latter was having a better run of opportunities, and he was quick to pot them. Although the day represented a danger to my wealth, I was enjoying it. The shooting was of vintage quality, and the chance to watch two dinosaurs locked in combat that at least one of them surely would have made mortal in another age was gripping, even if I had been foolish enough to underwrite one of the combatants.

After the fourth drive, young Preston read both sets of results out as the two were standing together, sounding like the teller on election night. "Thomas Makepeace Bradley," never knew about that silly middle name, I thought to myself "twenty-two birds off fifty-four shots. Alexander Augustus Bicester," that name's not much better "twenty-one birds off forty-one shots."

BUGGER! Again, while the moral victory lay with Alex, the numerical advantage remained with his rival. There was a big deficit to pull back, and indeed it had gone up by one during that drive. What to do? I'd got a cheat to the left of me, but what did the man to the right of me have in his bag?

The final drive was set in a curious place. Much further down the estate lay an old mill beyond a straggling fence. Once upon a time it must have been extensive, the heart of its own little area of creativity, but now it was forlorn and largely fallen. Built of large rectangular slabs of stone quarried locally, now greened with the moss of age and neglect, it was a great sprawling mess of tumbledownness. Still part roofed, it must have been forty yards from end to end. Like much of the estate, its purpose had been overtaken by time and technology.

However, even now the building was impressive. Forty feet high in places, the dead eyes of glassless frameless windows peered into the first intimations of dusk. It was girthed on the left and behind by a small plantation, and to the right by a broad stream. Now flowing limply, this stream would once have supplied the mill with its motive power. The birds would be in the plantation behind the old mill, obliviously sheltering and munching. At this point in the day, with the sun beginning to set over the Blankshire hills beyond, their thoughts would be leading towards roosting in the trees. For now, though, eating was their sole occupation. They had spent the last six months having each and every day made for them by humans, fed and sheltered. Now it was their turn to pay back.

The layout of the guns for the fifth drive was exactly as it had been six hours earlier. Everyone had moved a couple of spots after each drive, and as a result had come full circle. Alex was to the extreme left, and the belted earl far away to the right. The latter was slightly rattled, perhaps, but still clearly confident, not yet prepared to consider the possibility of defeat. After all, he had a lead of five. We were positioned some fifty yards from the old mill buildings, with the evening sun in our eyes. It was not the easiest of spots to shoot from, and probably wasn't supposed to be. We knew the birds would be high, high, high. Well, we had to have a finale to the little contest, and here was not a bad place.

As always at moments of high drama Albert was briefly here, chatting to his ennobled friend, then whoosh, roar, gone. Something, somewhere, was more urgent.

A little toot told us all to stand ready. Any quarry was now fair. Our hor d'oeuvres arrived, a fair showing of high flying wood pigeons, difficult shots all. We ignored them, although I was aware of the belted earl egotistically going through the motions of practising on them with his gun, showing us how fit and ready for the fight he was. Showoff, I thought.

Then the birds started to fly. Clearly between young Preston and Alex there was a determination to ensure we finished the day with a flourish, but realistically they were never going to please Nobody's Friend, as Albert had so memorably called the belted earl. However, I admired them in the nobility of their effort.

The noise of the guns echoed, "A ragged fusillade", to pinch a phrase that simply fitted the aural echoes that were washing over me. Aware as I was that the duel was of no great significance in the larger scheme of things, nonetheless if Alex could somehow contrive to win it would be hugely pleasing. That the belted earl would be annoyed beyond words contributed hugely to the enjoyment of the thought. Reverie and shooting go curiously well together. As Albert had explained so eloquently, the less focus there is on the matter at hand the better the co-ordination. However, attention, if not thought, was required. Suddenly the birds were coming thick and fast. I practiced my swing, chose my target and engaged with it. Again these were the best birds any shooting man could hope for: high, carried down on the wind, and, as a result, very fast. To shoot further in front than usual had to be the right thing.

Then, in the middle of my little self help exercise, I heard the beginnings of a furore. First I heard a shout, I wasn't sure from where. Was it important? I didn't know. A shooting day has much hullabaloo about it: dogs scampering; whistles blowing; directions being shouted; beaters crashing, purposefully whooping and a-hollering. I was focused, utterly concentrated on my own little word, but then…but then I looked. I could see half a dozen or so birds flying towards the far end of the line; birds much bigger than the average pheasant. White flashes of wings and heads, and spooky motionless but motionful flight. Lord, what were they? Whatever they were, they should not have been flying across the line.

Then, more commotion. A huge – under any other circumstances admirably huge – bouquet of pheasants now appeared. What were the shooters to do? Try their luck while the intruders remained in range, or restrain themselves? This looked complicated. I was angled across the sun and having problems telling what was going on; those at the end of the line would have the sun right in their eyes. Maybe they could only guess.

Suddenly, I heard the unmistakable call: "Twit twoo, twit twoo". This was not the late night meditative call of the hunting barn owl, but the call of an owl in distress. Whether it was from one of the birds or the guns I couldn't tell. I didn't know where the call was coming from, but it gave me a sudden insight into the nature of what was happening. Shots rang out from down the line; at least one gun seemed to be having a go regardless.

Damn and blast: owls! Where the hell had they come from? The old mill building, I guessed. The beaters might occasionally disturb a barn owl, but it would normally flit quietly away, its ghostly pale mien unnatural in the daylight. Gawd, I hoped no one had hit one. They'd be the laughing stock of the county – no, the whole of the shooting scene. These were experienced shooters; top of their game boys, born to this stuff. They would no more hit an owl than a Formula One driver would engage reverse while at the front of the grid – would they? It was simply not done; a social solecism beyond compare. The result? It would not bear thinking about. A lifetime of twit-twoos following one down the street; nudge nudges as one got on the bus, "Yes, dear, it's 'im, the owl murderer"; the butt of every Johnny-Cum-Lately's teasing on every shooting day from now until the grave. No, no one would be rash enough to shoot an owl.

I tried to focus while speculating. The big white-plumed birds had been very near the belted earl; they must have been roosting in the old mill. It was very unusual, but not unheard of, to see such a parliament of owls together. They had gathered to debate the merits of different sorts of mice as prey, no doubt, and had been upset by the sound of guns. I was puzzled as to why the keepers had not spotted them, but hell, the old mill was a big place. Dangerous to venture inside too I imagined.

Was it just an extraordinary coincidence they had commenced their sitting the day we passed through?

The birds, the proper ones with beautiful rainbow plumage rather than any other sort, continued thick and fast at our end of the line. While there was a hush from the far end, whatever was happening down there was not my problem. Alex clearly felt the same as he continued with his trigger happy and frighteningly accurate style. Young Preston, while he had one on eye on whatever drama was unfolding away from us, was still keeping count. This was his patch, after all.

Slowly the confusion down the line seemed to right itself. The shadows had drifted beyond range, and the natural order was restored. I slowed my swing; there was less to do now the birds were thinning out. The beaters appeared, now a scant hundred yards away, camouflaged shapes in the plantings behind the old mill.

I'd thought there could be little drama left in this dramatic day, but I had not allowed for young Preston and his showmanship. One last rank of previously hidden birds rose from behind the old mill itself, briefly fluttering above us, bent on escaping the crash and racket of the advancing beaters behind them. One final echo of gunshot reverberated and then the final trump, for today anyway.

Now to make sense of the earlier goings on. First, however, I bent pick up my discarded cartridge cases and pile them neatly for the "man wot does", who would surely appear in due course to tidy. Alex joined me, again unaware of my genteel considerations. People were paid to do such things, so why should he bother? Logical if one thought about it, although it wasn't very likely that he had.

"I do believe something a bit rum's been going on. I reckon my neighbour might just have had a pot shot or two at an owl, frightfully bad form."

"No, surely not. He wouldn't be that crass."

Young Preston walked down with us. "That went well for you, sir, another twenty-two birds off forty-one shots. I reckon we'll need to go back to when my dad was a lad to find shooting of that calibre." The glance in my direction was rather less impressed. "Think you were twelve off thirty-three, sir."

"Yes, yes, yes," said Alex, a picture of impatience now the tensions of the day, so beatifically ignored, suddenly overflowed his noble breast. "Let's go on and see what my neighbour's been up to. Hmmm, an owl, what?" As the bulk of the shooting party headed back to the gun bus, Alex and I walked in the opposite direction towards the belted earl.

Albert, with his nose for trouble, had at some point appeared at the far end of the drive. He was now addressing the belted earl in something less than respectful terms. "Well, well, well! Lordy, Lordy, oh Lordy, what 'ave you done?"

"I? Me? Done?" Clearly not used to being questioned in this rather less than reverential fashion, the earl was practically stuttering. "N-n-n-othing. I have done nothing, I tell you."

"Nothing, eh? Great puff of white nothing feathers I saw, was it? Reckon that parliament of owls is well and truly prorogued, my titled friend. A by-election might just be needed. We all saw 'em come this way, didn't we, lads? A puff of white feathers, something white splashing into the river..." Here Albert invited the opinions of the sheepish looking picker-uppers standing behind him, who stared busily at their feet; at their gun dogs; at the back of their hands. Sullen silence all around. This was not a conversation that they wished to be involved with – way above their pay grade.

Liversedge came over. "Well, all I can say is 'is Lordship was shooting well, then that ruddy parliament of owls appeared. Must of been eleven of 'em at least. Never seen so many gathered in one spot, great brutes." Gamekeepers seldom share the benevolent view of owls held by most of the population.

The conversation was beginning to take on a rather repetitive slant, until Albert broke the mould. "'Ow's the score, Livers ol' boy?"

"Well, 'is Lordship took seventeen off the drive, so that gives 'im ninety-seven in total."

"What, is that including or excluding the owl? 'Cos I reckon that should carry a penalty, 'ittin' a twit twoo."

The suggestion met a deafening silence, so Albert pressed on with the reckoning.

"And tell me, young Hey Presto, 'ow did Al do?"

"Well, sir, I've just totted it up. Lord Blankshire is on ninety-seven for the day too."

So now it was interesting, but Albert was not to be stymied. "So it's a draw, but what about the owl business?"

"Well..." stammered Liversedge, his look of awkwardness suggesting a certain lack of certainty, "I can't say as 'e did shoot an owl, and I can't say as 'e didn't."

"Twit twoo," murmured Albert. "Not our game, owls, are they, Lordy? Not really our bag. Bit uncertain, ain't we. The excitement, the rush of blood. One minute we're about to retain our lead, the next we're known in polite society as 'the owl murderer'. So the game is drawn. How's about that, M'Lord? Clear you've been thoroughly outshot, it is. Only that business with the ramblers that gave you any sort of lead. Now, how are we to settle this? Well now, it might suit us all if I were to confess to the most terrible attack of myopia. After all, that lot" Albert pointed to the keepers and picker-uppers, Liversedge nervously twisting his cap in hand to the fore "won't be saying anything to anyone of consequence. Not your sort, anyway, so that just leaves me: the only one 'oo was really watchin'. I 'ave been known to be the soul of discretion, but I 'ave also been known as a man of considerable persistence. I might, just might, take a walk along this 'ere stream bank to see what I can see." He paused, weighing his words slowly and with the appearance of care. "Of course," he said, glancing at the setting sun, "without further ado, twit twoo," here he grinned that foolish Albert grin that I had become so fond of, "we might just adjourn these proceedings. A little gracious concession from you, M'Lord?"

During the course of this maiden speech the earl had

stayed quiet, but his face had mottled. Now he joined his defence.

"No! What nonsense are you talking? Recount needed. Not my fault a bloody great swarm of…"

"Parliament, My Lord. Parliament – that's the technical term for a gathering of owls, as I'm sure that you, as a man with a seat in one, knows."

"Yes, yes, I know. Bloody things. What damn fool allowed…? Simply not fair. Some allowance is needed." At this point his face was developing an even greater ruddiness. He stared, his anger now contorting his features, and his shotgun loaded and unbroken in his hands. "Well the lot of you…" Both hands were on the gun as he looked for words to express the very devilish fury that was consuming him. "It's clear to me that you lot, and your bloody keepers… I mean to say, this is just beyond…" He slowly looked to all of us, the barrel of his gun raised, following his gaze.

I don't know what others thought, but to me this suddenly felt more than awkward. There was a violence in the air that was palpable. In the silence that fell, any humour in the situation had long vanished as the belted earl's fingers groped around the firing action of the gun.

Albert, sensing the situation, waved his hands. The belted earl suddenly coughed, shook his head, moved a finger, and the barrel of the gun collapsed, breaking limply downwards, finally powerless. Alex exhaled audibly. All too aware that limits had been reached, and that the barriers of etiquette and even more had been breached, he responded, anxious to defend the integrity of his keepers. Quietly but forcibly, all calm rationality, he dealt with the blustering, bullying manner of his neighbour.

"Sid, we'll have less gun waving if you don't mind. The old mill is a place where owls live, you know that. Their roost there is, after all, protected. You wouldn't expect me to ask my keepers to disturb them, would you? There is always the danger of one or two flying out of there, and it's unfortunate there were slightly more on this occasion. You of all people know that, Sid. Goodness knows, you've shot here often enough. To be honest, I think you've just got a bit carried away by that horrible desire of yours to win. Thing is, we're currently drawn even, and I actually have a better ratio of shots to birds. Are you telling me, after all this, you still want some sort of steward's enquiry?"

"'Course I am." The earl drew himself up to his full magnificence; at a little over six foot he could look annoyingly patrician, and even carried a touch of gravitas which seemed most inappropriate. "Of course I am," he repeated, with a hint of aggression in his voice. "Got to have clear rules, you know."

"Well, do you know what? I think Albert's right. He and I might just take ourselves off for a walk down the river. It's not a fast current, is it? Who knows what we might find being carried down stream, and if we find what I think we might find, and it ends up on the game cart, well...only one person at this end remotely near, and people do talk, don't they?"

Here Albert could restrain himself no longer. "It'd be awful, M'Lord, if you were to face the rest of your life not knowing, whenever you hear the distant twit twoo of a barn owl, whether it's the real thing or someone re-enacting this particular story all over again. Anyone for *The Barn Owl Sang In Berkeley Square?*"

Albert enunciated this particular prospect of social exclusion and mockery with great care, and the earl was again beside himself. All hint of patrician grandeur gone, he was red flushed with raw vulgar uncontrolled anger, but aware no words could change anything. The awful tendrils of defeat seeped into his conscious mind.

"Well all I can say is, you can take your damn day's shooting, and…"

"Yes!" said Albert, willfully misinterpreting the language. "Yes, we will take the day you promised. And don't forget the cheque for £2,000 you were also kind enough to offer, Lordy." As the angry belted earl flushed even brighter, Alex, ever the man of peace, offered a note of closure, clearly feeling that enough kicking of this particular man had taken place. "Do you know, Albert, we've had a long day. I think I'll take that as a yes. Do we really have the energy to walk down stream? I'm not sure we do, and, after all, the quality of Sid's word is often spoken of…"

Clearly on the wrong side of the argument, the belted earl was unable to resist vocalising a parting shot. "My dear old dad would be turning in his grave if he could see what was happening here today." With this, he turned on his heels.

As the solitary figure of the belted earl walked away, Alex observed, in a voice that would have undoubtedly carried to the retreating back, "Yes, his dear old dad would be turning, wouldn't he?" He paused. "Suspect he's obliged to do that most days, poor old fella!"

AFTERWORD

I<small>T WAS A</small> curious thing. Of course, I had to wonder at the coincidence of the parliament of owls and our assembly of peers. If it was more than a coincidence, the suspected perpetrator was not sharing. All I could get from Albert when I enquired as to the extent of his hand in the matter was an acknowledgement that, yes, it had turned out fine again, and a tapping of the Albert proboscis. "Shtuum" seemed to be the word of the hour. On the question of exactly what it was the earl had or had not shot in the heat of the moment, he was equally circumspect.

"Well, I did bring a few albino pheasants up for Hey Presto, as one keeper to another, you understand. Maybe it was one of those as was shot. But really, they're not for shooting either, just for novelty value. Of course, 'oo knows where Presto put 'em down. Anyway, he didn't ask me for precise coordinates. Sensible chap, that Presto quite likes 'im. Nope, the old earl, 'e got 'is just desserts if you ask me. 'E left without tipping the keepers. Shocking bad form, that. 'E wont be welcome again here, you mark my words."

I had a phone call from Alex a couple of days later. He'd had the usual stiff card of thanks from the belted earl, and from the envelope a cheque for £2,000 had fluttered to the floor. I gather Alex had jumped straight in his car and driven down to Upper Melsham. In his words, "Thought I'd better bang it in the bank double quick, before he had any second thoughts. Never know with that fella. Doing the right thing is just not his thing."

So the Blankshire county now had its great event to rally around. With the belted earl's offer of a prestige day of shooting heading the attractions, others could not resist being associated with the success. This meant a very long list of auction prizes and the county event of the year. People who would no more go hunting than they would do yak herding queued up to buy tickets, and if some of the wilder rumours were to be believed something of a lively grey market developed.

Lady Susan developed a renewed interest in life. The doorbell of the Big House once again rang frequently as the auction preparations built up, the place echoing to the faux chimes of Tom Jones' 'Delilah'.

I was swept aside by a variety of people anxious to be involved, although actually my role, the persuading and cajoling, had finished the moment the earl stalked away, angry and beaten. Even for him, the choice between pride and ostracism had not ultimately been that difficult, as William had so accurately foreseen.

Predictably, Lettice and the other members of the Ladies' Racquets Club led the charge, just as they had done for the book launch. With them finally fully on board, who could doubt the success of the auction?

My work was done. This meant my life could return to the pattern it had enjoyed before I so rashly accepted the gauntlet thrown down in such a cavalier fashion by Alex all those months before. I'd enjoyed my time hob-nobbing with the Blankshire great and good, but it was now time to return to what I really enjoyed: following the hounds wherever fate and the fox led them!

*

I look up from my desk. It's just after 9am, and in a little over an hour I will be meeting my old friend and compadre Col, complete with the resurrection wagon. Today we will be at a meet in an area of the county where we are now welcome for the first time in twenty years. Just south of the new Pinch-Me-Near-Forest nature reserve, called Pogle's Wood, the Blankshire will assemble for a proper day's hunting, untroubled by politics, owls or earls.

Lightning Source UK Ltd.
Milton Keynes UK
UKOW02f0701030516

273449UK00001B/21/P